FANG

Iron Devils MC

31 DAYS OF TRICK OR TREAT: BIKER AND MOBSTER

TICH BREWSTER

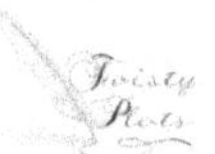

IRON DEVILS MC

FANG

ACKNOWLEDGMENTS

I want to thank all my readers for your continued support. You guys are awesome and mean the world to me. Big hugs and kisses to you all. Seriously, you have no idea how much it means to me.

A big thank you to Teresa and Shalisha for standing by my side on this crazy journey. You two have supported me from the beginning. I love you girls to the moon and back.

Christina and Kris are my rockstars. Those two do so much for me behind the scenes that allow me to spend more time behind the screen typing the words for your reading pleasure. Thank you, girls, for taking good care of me. XOXO

BLURB

A night filled with haunting thrills…

Winter is mourning what would have been. Being dumped on her birthday feels like the end of the world.

In the shadows of the carnival, Halloween brings unexpected magic when she crosses paths with Fang, a member of the Iron Devils MC. Dangerous, alluring, and full of mystery—Fang sparks a flicker of hope amid her misery.

With pasts overshadowed by pain, Fang and Winter find solace in one another.

As the dangers of Fang's life come to light, Winter must choose. Will she open her heart and let love in?

NOTE

This book is a work of fiction.
It is meant for entertainment purposes only.
Any inaccuracies within the pages are meant to enhance the
story.

CHAPTER ONE

Winter

Could today get any worse? Of course, that asshat had to do this on today of all days—my birthday. Staring at the text message on my phone, I blow out a frustrated breath and wipe away the lone tear that trails down my cheek.

BILLY:

> Hey, Win, I think it's time to see other people.

I didn't even get a *happy birthday*, just a *I think it's time to see other people* text. Last night he was telling me how much he loves me, and today he's breaking up with me. What a jerk. I can't believe I wasted two years with that idiot.

Ping. Ping. Ping.

Jelly's name flashes on the screen. Unlocking my cell phone, I open the text from my best friend.

JELLY:

You have got to see this.

The next text is a screenshot of Billy's social media post. It's a picture of him and Shelbi at Scoop Express, the ice cream place he took me to every Friday. His arm is around her shoulders, and the caption reads: *Out having a quick snack with my girl.* His girl? Seriously? We broke up less than five minutes ago.

JELLY:

I'm gonna kick his ass.

Pain like a thousand shards of glass slicing my heart forces me to my knees. I thought his stupid breakup text was bad. This is so much worse. How long has he been seeing Shelbi? Were they together while we were? A sob builds in my throat until I can't hold it back any longer.

Dropping my phone, I clutch my chest with one hand while falling forward onto the other. I feel dumb for crying over Billy. A man who treats me this way doesn't deserve my tears, yet I can't help but shed them.

Ping. Ping. Ping. Ping.

It's probably Jelly. I should text her back. If I don't, she'll just rush over here. The last thing I need is for her to come to my rescue when I know she's needed at work. Reaching for the device, I read her texts through the tears pooling in my eyes. Which is not an easy task, my friends.

JELLY:

Winter, are you okay?

JELLY:

Of course, you're not okay. What the hell
was I thinking. You need me to come over?

JELLY:

I should come over.

JELLY:

That's it, I'm calling in to work and coming
over.

Blinking the tears from my eyes, I tilt my head back and pinch the bridge of my nose. Will that stop the flow? I don't know, but it's worth a shot. I can't keep crying over someone who would toss me aside so easily.

Just as I knew she would, Jelly is going to ditch work to sit with me. I love her to death, but the last thing I feel like doing is having my best friend hold my hand. Having people feel sorry for me makes me feel like a burden. That's the last thing I want.

I think I'll tell her I'm good, then go dig the salted caramel ice cream out of the freezer and eat my feelings.

No. Go to work, I'm fine.

There is no response, so I assume she is on her way to work. Tossing my cell phone on the bed, I head to the kitchen for that salted caramel and a spoon. My heart is heavy, and my eyes have a steady stream of tears. It's official, today is the worst day of my life, and it's only a little after noon.

I hope Billy has a miserable life.

Is it too harsh to wish that on someone, especially someone who has been your boyfriend for the last two years? Maybe. Do I care? Hell no. That man just betrayed me in the worst way. I hope Karma comes and bites his ass good.

Kicking back in the recliner, I switch the TV on and scroll through movies. The minute Twilight fills the screen, I know this will be my heartbreak companion. I hit play and dig my spoon into the cold creaminess in the paperboard tub.

The sweet ice cream numbs my tongue and gives me brain freeze, but I welcome it. This sensation gives me something else to focus on. Even if it's only for a minute. Now, if it could numb my heart as well, then I'd be set.

Once the pain in my head dissipates, I scoop another spoonful. Just as I open wide for another bite, my front door swings open. I scream because I was not expecting anyone. Jelly strolls in like she owns the place and hangs her purse on the coatrack.

My best friend treks across the room, takes the spoon from my hand, and shoves it in her mouth. We've been best friends for as far back as I can remember, eating and drinking after one another is no biggie. "If you're going to sit here and wallow in self-pity, I'm joining you."

"Uh, no, you're not." I snatch the spoon from her hand. "You have work."

"Screw work." She slides into the oversized chair with me. "It will still be there tomorrow. Trust me, they have it covered."

This is why Jelly is my person. No matter what I'm going through, if I need her, she's there. She's a no-questions-asked, ride or die, I've got your back kind of friend. Angelica Myers, aka Jelly, is my rock in times of need. The one I trust with my very life.

A tub of ice cream and a package of Oreos later, Jelly is dragging me from my cozy recliner. She is totally ruining my Edward vibe, but does she care? Nope, not even a little. "Come on, Winter, you cannot wallow all day. It's your birthday for crying out loud, and our favorite holiday. The bikers are hosting this year's Halloween Carnival. We are not going to miss this."

I do my best to tug free, but my bestie has an iron grip on my wrist. "Jelly, seriously, I don't feel like celebrating tonight." Once we enter my bedroom, she releases me and heads straight for the closet. When I see her reaching for my costume, I freak. "No," I shout.

Jumping back, my best friend turns on her heels, eyes wide. "What the hell, Win?"

"Sorry." Damn, my emotions are out of control. "I am not wearing that. That's the Bonnie to Billy's Clyde."

Jelly rips the costume from the hanger. "Then we're burning this shit." She storms from the room, yelling over her shoulder. "We'll go shopping."

"I'd rather not." I follow her to the kitchen, where she deposits the Bonnie outfit into the trash.

"It's not up for debate." Her phone beeps, and she pulls it from her back pocket to check the text message. With a frown, she types a quick reply and shuts off the device. "Get some shoes on, we're getting you all sexy for tonight."

Sexy? What the hell is she talking about? "What's this all about?"

"Nothing." It's not nothing, I can see it in her eyes. There's a fire there that wasn't before. It can only be about one person. Billy.

Just the thought of him causes my stomach to twist in knots. Again. "What was that text about?"

"You don't want to know." Nodding her head toward my bedroom, she says, "Get some shoes and let's bounce."

Getting out of the house will do me good, I know it will. So, instead of resisting, I trek to my room for shoes. My cell phone lies on the bed. I totally forgot about it. Funny how heartache can do that to a person. Because I can't seem to help myself, I open social media and check Billy's posts.

The first post I see is of him and Shelbi sitting on the hood of his car, kissing. Like a glutton for punishment, I continue scrolling. Photo after photo of the two of them. Though it hurts to look, I can't seem to stop myself from clicking on each photo and zooming in. Billy may have stuck the knife in my heart, but I'm the one who keeps twisting the blade.

Sliding on a pair of shoes, I grab my purse and sling it over my shoulder. Jelly is standing by the front door. Turmoil must be evident on my face because she wraps her arms around me in a bear hug. "It'll be okay, Win. I promise." Ushering me out the door, she adds, "And I will kick his ass seven ways to Tuesday, just say the word."

"As much as I'd love that, it's not necessary." What would it solve anyway? It would only bring me a sliver of happiness, and it wouldn't last long. So, why bother? Besides, he's the kind of guy who would send her to jail for delivering a slice of justice.

There's a look in my best friend's eyes. One I can't quite decipher, and I wonder what she is up to. With Jelly, there's no telling. She could already have a hitman on his way to Billy's. Okay, that's a bit extreme. My bestie would never hire another person to commit murder. That's not her style. Yet, I have to wonder what it is she's done.

CHAPTER TWO

Fang

What the hell did I get roped into? Carnival games, candy, pop music, and costumes. Sinner has lost his damn mind, signing us—and by us, I mean the Iron Devils MC—up to host the Halloween Carnival. I hate these loud, obnoxious games, the cringy pop music, and the god-awful costumes. The only good thing about this place is the endless supply of Snickers.

I wonder if Sinner would notice if I took off.

Just as I turn to make my escape, Sinner steps out from behind the kissing booth. "Not thinking about running off, are ya?"

How does this man know every move before I even make it? It's like he's a wizard or something. "No, of course not."

The grin that crosses his face says that he doesn't buy my lie. Honestly, I didn't expect him to. The man is president, or Prez as we call him, of the Iron Devils. He can smell a lie a mile away. Good thing Sinner is my uncle, otherwise the man may have cut off my balls and fed them to me. "Good, I want you overseeing the Haunted House."

Great, just what I had hoped for, screaming girls running around in the dark. Somebody shoot me now.

"Oh, Ramon is bringing you a costume." Just as I open my mouth to protest—because let's face it, I haven't worn a Halloween costume since I was ten years old—Sinner pins me with a hard glare. "Wear the damn costume, that ain't a request."

Well, screw me. Just as Sinner enters the tent where the fortune teller is set up, Ramon strides up next to me, wearing a shit-eating grin. This can only mean one thing. Sinner left him in charge of picking out my costume. He better not have picked out some fairy wings. I'm not dressing in some froufrou shit.

"Found the perfect costume for you." Ramon shoves the bag into my hand.

Opening the bag, I peer at the contents. Well, that's not as bad as I thought it would be. I pull the black wings out. There are elastic straps to fit around my arms. Okay, I can handle this. No big deal. That is, until I see that there is nothing else inside the bag. "Where's the rest?"

Ramon's smirk does not sit well with me. Between the look Sinner gave me and Ramon's, I'm fairly certain I will not appreciate this little costume they picked out for me. "That's it."

I shrug. "Cool, so I'll wear a black shirt and blue jeans."

"You wish." Ramon slaps me on the back. "The blue jeans, sure, but no to the shirt. Since this carnival is twenty-one and older, Sinner said that tonight's costumes are adult-themed."

Of course, my uncle, the horndog. There is no way in hell I am dressing as some sexy fallen angel. Nope, ain't happening. "Uh, uh." I toss the wings back into the bag and hand them out to Ramon. "You wear it."

"Unlike you, I have no problem strutting my stuff." He pushes the bag back toward me. "But I have my own fallen angel wings." With those parting words, Ramon is off to join Sinner in the fortune teller's tent.

Looks like I will have to swallow my pride and showcase half my body. Why? Because you don't disobey the Prez. Bad things happen to those who violate a direct order. That does not exclude his own flesh and blood. What Sinner says, goes. Period. I did not work my ass off as a prospect and become a patched member of the Iron Devils just so I can spit in the club's face and get my ass handed to me.

At least I don't have much of a wardrobe change. All I have to do is remove my cut and my shirt, slip on these massive black wings, and I'm done. I'm already in a pair of faded blue jeans. If only my brother could see me now. He'd laugh his ass off at the sight of me in this getup.

Just thinking of Justin is stirring up feelings I've been trying my best to bury. It's bringing about hatred, anger, and hurt. So much hurt. Justin is...was my younger brother. Protecting him was my number one priority, and I screwed up.

Pinching the bridge of my nose, I shake off the bad

memories. A lot of good therapy did me. I can't even think of my brother without wanting to go postal. The pain is so bad I can't even keep his photo up in my room.

It's not that I want to forget him. I don't. But seeing him and knowing he's gone because I failed him destroys me. My brother was only twenty-three years old when he was shot in the back. He had his whole life ahead of him. A steady girlfriend. Okay, so we shared the girlfriend, but he still loved her. Now it's all gone. All of it.

So lost in my thoughts, I don't hear Sinner approach. When he lays a hand on my shoulder, I spin, fists up. "Whoa, Fang." My uncle picks up the black wings I must have dropped. Taking a good look at me, he blows out a breath. "Let me guess, you're thinking about Vile?"

Vile is Justin's club name. We all have one. None of us goes by our legal names.

"Listen, kid, you can't let Vile's death tear you up forever. At some point, you're gonna have to forgive yourself. He'd want you to." Sinner tosses the wings at me. "Have no doubt, when the time is right, we will avenge Justin's death. You have my word on that. My nephew deserves justice."

CHAPTER THREE

Winter

Wouldn't you know it, Jelly took me shopping for a costume and ended up buying a sexy nurse outfit despite my protests. Okay, if I'm being honest, I didn't put up much of a fight. Earlier, I saw Billy's post about hitting up the carnival with his new girl, and I'm secretly hoping he sees me there. I want him to see what he's missing.

"No, girl." Jelly shakes her head. We're at her place getting ready for the carnival. Ducking into her closet, she digs around until she finds what she's looking for. "Ah, these are perfect." Dangling from her fingers is a silver pair of stilettos. "Here, wear these."

I glance down at my flats. "But these are comfy." Walking around in stilettos all night will absolutely kill my feet.

"Girl, it's not about comfort." Tossing the heels next to me, she stands at the mirror and applies red lipstick. "Tonight is about being sexy and showing that asshole what he left behind."

Sorry, feet, sexiness is our number one priority tonight. Slipping into the heels, I test them out. It's been years since I've worn heels, and never any with this much height. The first thing I notice is the strain on my ankles. Jeez, this might be a long night. As I walk, I'm embarrassed to say that I'm almost as wobbly as a newborn horse.

Let's just hope I don't trip and fall.

After Jelly applies lipstick to my lips, she's ready to rock and roll. The carnival is being held at the fairgrounds on the outskirts of town. It's not a long drive, around fifteen minutes. As we're turning into the parking lot, I suddenly worry about how short this skirt is. I'm not one to reveal too much skin. Being an author, I'm usually walking about in sweatpants.

"Stop fretting and get out. We have a night of fun ahead of us." Jelly unbuckles my seatbelt and motions for me to get out.

Taking a deep breath, I open the car door and exit the vehicle. My eyes constantly scan the lot for any signs of Billy's car. Even though I want him to see me all sexed up, I'm afraid of what seeing him with *her* will do to me.

Breathe, Winter, it'll be okay.

I'm not convinced it will be. In fact, I'm pretty sure that once I see him, it won't be. Tonight's plans didn't come with an exit strategy in the event I run into my ex. Walking across the parking lot in these heels is a sight, and not a good one.

Jelly is kind enough to loop her arm through mine when I nearly tumble to the ground.

Once we reach solid ground, my balance is better, and she untangles herself from me to dig through her purse. The man at the gate is tall, bulky, and looks like he'd rather be anywhere other than here. His reddish blonde beard is braided, and he's dressed as a Viking. Of their own accord, my eyes travel down to his bare chest, where his nipples are standing loud and proud.

"ID." His eyes land on me, and he smirks when he notices where my gaze had been. Jelly and I fish out our IDs and hand them over. Giving them a once-over, he hands them back. "Have fun." Turning, he points to the men standing on either side of the gate. "See the guys for your courtesy drink."

Courtesy drink? What kind of carnival did Jelly drag me to?

Ushering me to the right side of the gate, she gets two shots from a guy wearing a Santa outfit, minus the red coat. I glance over at the man on the opposite side. He's also shirt-less. "Jelly, what kind of carnival is this?" She giggles but otherwise says nothing.

Mr. Bare-chested Santa chuckles and glances at my best friend. "You didn't tell her you were bringing her to a Biker Carnival?"

"Oh, I did." She downs her shot and hands me mine. "I just didn't elaborate on the fact that it's twenty-one and up."

Okay, twenty-one and up is no big deal. Though it doesn't explain the shirtless men at the entrance. Bringing the shot glass to my lips, I tip it and down the contents. A burn trails down my throat, and I suck air through my teeth. Damn, that's straight up tequila.

Taking the empty plastic shot glass from me, Mr. Santa says, "You ever been to a Biker event, babe?" I shake my head. "Well, tonight's carnival is adult-themed. Don't be surprised if you see a little bumpin' and grindin', if ya know what I mean."

"Wait, what?" But before he can say more, Jelly takes me by the hand and tugs me through the crowd. As I glance over my shoulder, I see the Santa biker chuckling. Then he winks at me before handing the next in line their drink.

"Don't worry." Jelly bumps her hip into mine, nearly causing me to trip in these crazy shoes. "It's not as bad as what you're imagining. I promise."

"But he said—" Now I almost wish I had stayed home. Almost.

"Forget what he said. Will the occasional couple be having a quicky behind a building? Yeah, for sure. This is a Biker event. Of course, that's going to include sexual behavior. But it will not be out in the middle of the festivities."

I'm still unsure if this is where I want to be, but we're here, so we may as well have fun. Right?

As we enter the festivities, I see normal carnival things. Games tables, rides, vendors, a haunted house, corn maze, haunted hayrides, and I see there's even a costume contest. We stop at the ticket booth and pay for the night pass bracelet, which will allow us unlimited access to every ride.

Of course, the first ride I want to hop on is the haunted roller coaster. Luckily for me, the line for this one is fairly short. As I look around, I notice that every ride is manned by what appears to be a Biker. You guessed it, every single one of them is bare-chested. I'm seeing the theme, and now I understand why Jelly picked a sexy nurse costume for me.

Once the ride comes to a stop and people start to exit, we're ushered on. It's been so long since I've ridden a roller coaster, I'm a little nervous. An older man with muscles for days comes to strap me in. On his right pec, I see the word *SINNER* tattooed. He's dressed in tight Wranglers, cowboy boots, and a cowboy hat. Holstered to his hip is a gun. I sure hope it's fake. Especially with all the drinking that appears to be going on.

Interesting.

"Enjoy the ride, darlin'." He tests the bar to make sure it's secure, then moves on to the next car. Cowboy Biker takes his spot at the control panel and speaks into the microphone. "Get ready for the scariest roller coaster of your life."

Without warning, he hits the switch, and we begin our ascent. It's slow, and our car jerks as it climbs the track. Once we reach the top and I see the drop, my stomach twists. That's a mighty steep drop-off.

Jelly lifts her hands in the air once we start picking up speed. Screaming fills the air as passengers experience that swift drop. I can see the tunnel at the bottom. There is nothing but pure black from where I'm sitting.

When we fully descend and enter said tunnel, the car jerks to a near stop. It slowly moves through the darkness. Flashes of blue lights. Echoes of laughter, and not the happy kind. This laughter is of the creepy clown kind. The kind that makes the hairs on your arms stand on end.

A hand caresses my arm. At first, I think it's Jelly. Then I realize that it's coming from the outside. Someone I can't see is touching me. When the blue light flashes again, I see a dark figure moving away from the tracks.

As we move along, there are other jump scares. A Jason mask that suddenly glows red with the theme song. Large spiders that fall toward the moving cars. The sound of a chainsaw starting. What feels like creepy crawlies on the back of the neck when it's pitch black.

When the doors swing open and light filters in, I breathe a sigh of relief. My heart is pounding so hard I can hear it in my ears. We exit, and I grip the metal railing to steady myself. That ride was intense. I wasn't expecting that. Whoever put that together knows how to play on one's senses. It was scary, and at times I felt like I might pass out.

"Ooh, I see a haunted house." Jelly tugs on the sleeve of my top.

Another one? I'm not sure my heart is ready for round two of haunted attractions. "I don't know. How about some food or something first?"

"Are you kidding me?" She shakes her head. "There's plenty of time for food later. Look at that line." I do. Compared to all the other attractions, this line is by far the shortest. "Let's walk through and then eat. Come on." Grabbing hold of my hand, she begins to drag me toward the house.

"Fine." At least we'll be on foot in there.

A man dressed as Thor is letting people in by groups of six. I notice that he flirts with every girl who passes him. As each group is let in, we move further up the line. Until we're standing at the head. Thor winks at me as he takes a step toward us. "Naughty nurse, I like."

I can't help but roll my eyes. What a shameless flirt with zero regard for one's boundaries. "Have you used that line on every female that's come through here?"

"You jealous?" A smirk lifts one side of his mouth.

"Hardly." Why would I be jealous over a man who shows zero signs of commitment? All his actions do is remind me of my ex and his cheating ways. Okay, I don't exactly know that he cheated on me. Billy could have just been interested in Shelbi before, but didn't make a move until this morning. I highly doubt it, but it's possible.

Pressing a finger against the earpiece, he says, "Roger that." Then we are ushered through the door along with the three guys behind us.

It's pitch-black inside, and I immediately reach for Jelly's hand. Blue light flashes, and I see a bald man with smudges around his eyes. At first, he's across the room, but when the light flashes again, he is right in my face. That's not what causes me to scream. No, I let out a shrill noise because in that flash, I see him place a rat on my shoulder.

Oh God, is it alive? Yes, I think it is, I can feel it crawling from one shoulder to the other. Eww, I hate rats. This critter better not bite me. I will seriously throw hands if I end up with puncture wounds in my neck. Laughter sounds right next to my ear. This creep is still next to me.

When the lights flash again, he's gone, and so is the rat. Thank the good Lord.

Moving on to the next room, my stomach drops when I see that this one is a suicide scene. A guy is sitting in a chair with a gun in his mouth. He's crying around the barrel, mumbling something about a breakup and wanting to leave this world behind.

Just when I think he's going to pull the trigger, his eyes flick toward the guy standing behind me. With an evil smirk, he removes the barrel from his mouth and slowly aims his weapon at the person standing next to me.

Standing, his long legs stride toward us. Not knowing what is happening is rapidly increasing my heartrate. Surely this is a prop gun. Right? Jelly wouldn't have brought me to a carnival with questionable activities. I know her better than that, and judging by the way she's clutching my hand, I'd say she's just as surprised as I am.

The psycho with the gun stops directly in front of me, his weapon still aimed at the man who is now trying to worm his way behind me, making me his shield. What a coward. The gun tips upward and the actor shakes his head. "You're a pussy, what kind of man uses a woman as a shield?" Nodding toward an open door, he says, "Get out of here before I decide to tie you up and keep you as prisoners."

Each remaining room is more interactive than the last. On more than one occasion, I wonder if my life is truly in danger. Whoever these bikers are, they sure know how to scare the life out of a person. I'm starting to wish I had just stayed home tonight.

When the back door opens and the carnival noises filter into the room, I breathe a sigh of relief. Yes, I love horror movies. Yes, I love scary attractions. But tonight was on a whole new level of fright.

The coward who hid behind me in room two shoves me

out of the way, exiting the haunted house. I lose my footing and stumble into a man wearing big black wings. His dark hair is a right mess. It looks like he may have been running his fingers through it recently.

Gripping me by the shoulders, he steadies me. Those brown orbs pierce through me, down to the depths of my soul. "You okay?"

CHAPTER FOUR

Fang

The carnival is in full swing, and to be honest, I didn't expect to see so many adults out tonight. When I think of a carnival, I think of endless kid activities and screaming children. I'm walking around, overseeing—as my uncle put it—the haunted house. To be honest, I'm bored as all get out. I'd rather be at the bar. Hell, I'd rather be sitting on my bed with nothing to do.

Ramon nods at me when I glance over at the kissing booth. He is happily planting his lips on every girl who steps up to the booth. He's even taken pictures with a couple of them. That man is having the time of his life tonight.

Wish I could say the same.

We are letting in groups of six. The haunted house is set

up into five rooms, each of which has a gory scene. Unbeknownst to the guests, each room is interactive. No, we don't do anything that would harm a guest, but we do give them the scare of a lifetime.

The back door flies open, and a group of girls comes running out, holding onto each other and screaming loud enough to wake the dead. I glance at my watch. Not even nine o'clock. Good lord, will this night ever end?

A man dressed as Dracula flaps his cape as he walks by, shouting, "I vant to suck your blood," as he rushes up to a blonde and bends her at the waist, planting his mouth on the side of her neck. She squeals and he tightens his grip, bringing their bodies flush together.

As long as she's not protesting, I'm not getting involved.

When I trek toward the front of the line, two of the women standing there bat their eyelashes at me. The redhead reaches out and runs her hand down my abs. Her fingers are chilly from the cooling night air, and it elicits goosebumps on my flesh.

"Not right now, sugar," I tell her.

Sticking out her bottom lip, she uses what she probably thinks is a seductive voice. It's not. "Come on, Mr. Fallen Angel, surely you can spare a few minutes." Looking around, she smiles when she finds the corn maze. "I'm sure we can find a private spot out in the corn field."

"I'm sure we could." Removing her hand from my body, I step just out of her reach so I can talk to Zero. "You got this handled for a few? I need to step away from all the screaming for a minute."

Zero nods. "Sure thing, Fang."

"Fang?" The handsy redhead smiles. "I'll let you sink your fangs into me anytime."

"I bet you would." Turning on my heel, I stalk off. Away from the overly dramatic women inside the haunted house. What I need is a smoke. As I stroll through the carnival, I dig my pack of cigarettes from my front pocket.

Just as I flick my Zippo and bring the flame toward the cigarette, a small hand curls around my arm. I glance down at the petite girl clinging to me. Her black hair has bright orange highlights in it. It kind of reminds me of flames licking at the night air. "Please, just go with it."

Furrowing my brow, I'm about to ask her what she means when she lifts up on tiptoes, rips the cigarette from my mouth, and plants her lips on mine. Thank god I have enough sense in me to close my Zippo, so I don't set her pretty hair aflame.

It's clear that she is putting on a show, most likely to make a boyfriend jealous, because her lips don't move against mine. She is perfectly still and looking over my shoulder. Well, this won't do. If she wants to make some guy jealous, then we're going to make him good and jealous. Stuffing my Zippo back in my pocket, I cup the back of her head and open my mouth against hers.

There's a small gasp when I poke my tongue out and run it along her bottom lip. Her eyes shoot to mine and widen. "I'm going with it, baby." With my free hand, I grab her ass and squeeze. "You gonna join in on the fun?" I ask against her lips.

Footsteps grow louder behind me. This gets her attention, and she glances behind me. Wrapping her arms around my neck, she opens her mouth, and I take the opportunity to slide my tongue inside. She tastes like barbeque and margarita. An odd combination, but one I'm thoroughly enjoying. Only because it's on her, my little siren.

A small moan slips from her throat, and she runs her fingers through my hair. Gripping her thighs, I lift her, and she automatically wraps her legs around my waist. The carnival and the crowd fade as we kiss. All I know in this moment is the feel of this nameless woman in my arms.

"Winter?" The man's voice is grating on my nerves.

Winter, is that her name? Her name matches the spearmint gum I love to chew. At the sound of her name coming from this man's mouth, Winter stiffens in my arms. Her tongue stops moving against mine.

She breaks the kiss, resting her head on my shoulders for a brief second before untangling her legs from my waist. Setting her down on her feet, I gaze into her hazel pools. Agony reflects back at me. I don't know who this man is, but he put that dimness in her eyes, and I want to punch him in the throat for hurting her.

"I've got you," I whisper into her ear. There's a slight tremble to her body and she nods her head. Wrapping my arms around her, I glance over at the prick. Ain't nothing special about him. He's lean, but there's not an ounce of muscle on him. Just a basic male who doesn't care what his body looks like. "Can I help you?"

"Yeah, you can leave so I can talk to my girl."

In the distance, I can see a blonde glaring daggers at us. She crosses her arms and pops out a hip. Well, well, well. Looks like this guy here is a Romeo. I'll have fun knocking him off his throne. "Doesn't look like she's your girl to me, seeing as she's in my arms and the taste of her still lingers in my mouth."

Nostrils flaring, he takes a step toward me. "Listen here, I don't know who you think you are—"

Funny, he doesn't have a clue who I am. Of course, many don't recognize us without our cuts. Being without them is a very rare occurrence. We wear those like it's a second skin. We're proud of who we are and where we come from. "I'm gonna stop you right there." No need to make a scene, Sinner will kill me if I do. "Looks like you have a girl over there that wants your attention. Why don't you leave us alone?"

Ignoring me, he turns his attention to the woman currently burying her face in my shoulder. "Winter?"

Her chest expands against my bare flesh when she inhales. I swear it's like she is preparing to face the devil. If only she knew who the real devil was. Stepping out of the confines of my embrace, Winter turns to face the prick standing before us. To my satisfaction, she loops her arm through mine, and his eyes follow the movement.

"What do you want, Billy?" She says his name with such disdain, it makes me wonder what the asshole did to her.

Billy waves his hand in my direction. "What are you doing, Winter? This isn't like you."

"Not like me?" Winter's arm tightens around mine, like she needs my strength to have this conversation. "Look, Billy, what I do and who I choose to do it with is no longer your concern. If you recall, you broke up with me by text this morning."

"I know, but—" He doesn't get the chance to finish that

sentence because Winter straightens her spine and speaks over him.

"You texted me this morning that we should see other people. You broke up with me on my frickin' birthday." Wait, today is her birthday, and this loser dumped her on her special day. Unbelievable. Snuggling into my side, she cups my jaw with her free hand. "You didn't want me, so I found someone who does."

"Oh yeah, you found a new man in less than twelve hours?" Crossing his thin, undefined arms, he says, "That's rich."

"Considering you posted a picture of you and *your girl,*" she almost snarls the words, your girl, "just seconds after you sent that cowardly breakup text, I'd say that statement defines you quite well."

When Billy reaches for Winter, I snag him by the wrist and squeeze. Those pathetic brown eyes of his widen in fear. Yeah, you'd better fear me. You cross me and I will rain hell down on you so fast you won't know what hit you. "I think it's time you get the hell away from Winter. Ya hear me?"

CHAPTER FIVE

Across from the haunted house is a barbeque truck. Jelly and I are sharing a plate of barbeque nachos and hot links. I can't seem to get the dark-haired fallen angel out of my head. When he reached out to steady me, I nearly pushed up on my toes to plant my lips on his.

If I had, it wouldn't have been a big deal. I'm no longer taken. Billy set me free, which means I can kiss whoever I want.

Jelly lifts her hand and summons one of the men working the cash bar. He is wearing white wings and a halo. Yet I doubt he is anything resembling angelic. Especially with that devilish grin. "What can I get you ladies?"

"Margaritas, don't go easy on the tequila." Jelly hands him cash.

When he returns, he hands her a napkin with a phone number, presumably his. "Let me know if you need anything else."

Lifting the plastic cup, I lick the salt, then sip the ice-cold margarita. That bartender sure did not skimp on the tequila. I'm pretty sure it's ninety-nine percent alcohol. Damn, that stuff is stout. I may need to order more food to absorb the contents of my cup.

Just as I stab a hot link and lift it to my lips, I hear a high-pitched giggle. I look over and immediately drop my fork. It's no surprise to see him here, but knowing I'd run into him and actually running into him are two different things.

Billy's hand is squeezing Shelbi's ass, and his tongue is so far down her throat I'm amazed she isn't choking on it. Jelly's gaze follows mine and she stands. "Are you kidding me?" Marching over to them, she grabs a handful of Billy's hair.

Wide eyes fall on my best friend. "Jelly, what the hell?" Then his eyes lock with mine. "Win?"

Before either of us can process what's going on, Jelly lets go of his hair and punches him square in the nose. Shelbi screams, Billy groans, and Jelly shouts. She's angry at him for the way he dumped me and immediately moved on.

This is all too much. I can't stick around and watch. My heart is a jumbled mess right now. Seeing him hurts. Seeing him with *her* is like a knife to the heart. I know my best friend is defending me, but even that is too much.

I need to get out of here before I break down.

Jumping up from the chair, I take off running in the opposite direction. Which happens to be toward the haunted house. I can hear Billy calling after me, and Jelly telling him off. When I hear heavy footfalls behind me, I know exactly who it is. It's confirmed when Shelbi yells, "Billy, where are you going?"

I veer to the left. Billy is starting to catch up with me, and that fact sends panic through me. Now is not the time to face that man. Like a beacon, my eyes zero in on a pair of large black wings.

Could it be the same guy who kept me from falling earlier?

Hoping he doesn't think I'm completely nuts, I rush up to him and grab hold of his arm. The muscles in his arm flex. Then his gaze slowly lowers, recognition shining in those brown pools. I can hear Billy getting closer. Throwing caution to the wind, I prepare myself for what I'm about to do.

Mr. Fallen Angel lifts an eyebrow, probably wondering what the hell I'm up to. Praying he isn't in a relationship, I say, "Please, just go with it."

Furrowing his brows, he opens his mouth to speak. Before he can question me on my strange behavior, I stand on tiptoes, rip the cigarette from his mouth, and press my lips to his. The sound of his Zippo snapping shut barely registers. I'm so caught up in the feel of his smooth lips.

Though my lips are on his, I'm not making a move to actually kiss him. I mean, what if he's not single? Well, if he is taken, I suppose I've already put him in a serious predicament. Any woman seeing her man lip-locked with another woman wouldn't care if there was no actual kissing. All she would see is her man kissing another woman.

Shit. Please be single.

Footsteps slow and a huff leaves Billy's lips. I look over my fallen angel's shoulder—well, as best as I can considering his height—and see my ex standing with his arms crossed and a scowl on his face.

Fallen Angel—I really wish I knew his name—slips his Zippo in his pocket. I'm a little taken aback when he cups the back of my head and opens his mouth against mine. I gasp when his tongue glides along my lower lip.

With wide eyes, I look up at the man I'm currently lip-locked with. I didn't expect this. To answer my unspoken question, he says, "I'm going with it, baby." One hand still cupping my head, his other grabs my ass and squeezes. "You gonna join in on the fun?" His words are spoken against my mouth.

Footsteps grow louder, and I glance back at Billy, who is moving closer to us. Not knowing what else to do, I wrap my arms around this guy's neck. Deciding it's time to join in the fun, as he put it, I open my mouth.

Taking that as an invitation, he slips his tongue in. Spearmint and beer invade my senses. On anyone else, I would be turned off, but on him, I want more. A small moan slips from me, and I run my fingers through his hair.

I'm surprised by my behavior. This isn't like me.

Releasing my head, he grips both of my thighs, lifting me off my feet. Reflexively, I wrap my legs around his waist. The sounds of the carnival fade in the background as we kiss. A kiss I can't seem to get enough of.

"Winter?" Billy sounds hurt, though I don't know why.

When his voice breaks through my bliss, I stiffen. Shame fills my heart and my tongue stills. Slowly, I break the kiss and rest my head on my fallen angel's shoulder for just a second before untangling my legs from his waist.

Setting me back on my feet, his brown pools gaze into my hazel ones. I know he can see the turmoil I'm in. I'm not good at hiding my emotions. Tracing my lips with his thumb, he leans in and whispers, "I've got you."

There's no stopping the tremble that snakes through my body. For reasons I can't explain, I trust this nameless man to protect me from the one who shattered my heart this morning. I nod and he wraps his arms around me. Why do I feel safe in the arms of a stranger?

He turns his head to engage with my ex. "Can I help you?"

Billy's nasally voice brings a smile to my lips. A smile, because I know that the only reason he sounds like that is because Jelly punched him good. "Yeah, you can leave so I can talk to my girl."

My girl? Did Jelly punch him so hard that he forgot what he did this morning? Wetness trails down my cheeks. Am I crying? I can't let Billy see that he's affecting me this badly. To my relief, my safe haven, AKA the fallen angel, tightens his hold on me and shifts us so my back is to my ex. Completely shielding me from his prying eyes. "Doesn't look like she's your girl to me, seeing as she's in my arms and the taste of her still lingers in my mouth."

The sound of Billy breathing heavy carries above the carnival noises. "Listen here, I don't know who you think you are—"

I feel his chuckle against my cheek. "I'm gonna stop you right there." It's funny how this man that I literally just met, has defended me more than my ex. Kind of makes me wonder why the hell I was with Billy to begin with. "Looks like you have a girl over there that wants your attention. Why don't you leave us alone?"

"Winter?" Billy's tone is hurt.

Yeah, cry me a river. You hurt me first.

Inhaling deeply, I mentally count to ten before stepping out of the comfort of my defender's embrace. When I turn around, the first thing I see is Shelbi standing in the distance, watching us with her arms crossed. I can't be here, not with Billy. Looping my arm around my new friend's, I finally look my ex in the eyes. "What do you want, Billy?"

Waving a hand toward the man whose arm I'm clinging to, Billy asks, "What are you doing, Winter? This isn't like you."

"Not like me?" Anger and hurt war inside my heart. I want to lash out, but I can feel the tears wanting to break free. If only I had the strength for this. "Look, Billy, what I do and who I choose to do it with is no longer your concern. If you recall, you broke up with me by text this morning."

"I know, but—" That pathetic look on his face grates my nerves something fierce.

Speaking over him, I decide to put an end to this conversation so I can get the hell out of here. "You texted me this morning that we should see other people. You broke up with me on my frickin' birthday." Snuggling into my savior's side, I place a hand on his jaw, gazing up at him, but speaking to Billy. "You didn't want me, so I found someone who does."

"Oh yeah," Billy sniggers. "You found a new man in less than twelve hours?" Then he huffs. "That's rich."

The audacity. "Considering you posted a picture of you

and *your girl* just seconds after you sent that cowardly breakup text, I'd say that statement defines you quite well."

When Billy reaches for me, I flinch. But what surprises me is the fact that the man whose embrace I've been in snags Billy by the wrist, squeezing. My ex's brown eyes widen in fear. I should probably be frightened as well, but I'm not. If anything, it makes me feel that much safer. "I think it's time you get the hell away from Winter. Ya hear me?"

Billy whimpers but nods. No other words are spoken. My ex hightails it to his new girlfriend and the two of them walk away. Finally, I can breathe. Twisting my hands in front of me, I thank the man for helping me get rid of my ex. "Thank you for that."

"No problem." Those brown pools soften as he gazes down at me. "Listen, I gotta get back to my post, but let me treat you to some birthday pancakes later."

Because this man is captivating, I find myself agreeing to birthday pancakes. "Yeah, that sounds good."

"Great." He holds out his hand. "Let me see your phone." I lift a brow in question. "So, I can call you. My shift ends in thirty minutes."

"Oh, okay." Slipping my cell phone from the tiny pocket on this short skirt, I hand it over. He inputs his information, texts himself, then hands it back. Glancing down, I chuckle at the name he put as his contact. "Fang?"

"Yeah." He pinches my chin.

"Seriously, you put Fang as your contact name."

He laughs. "That's my name."

"Your mother named you Fang?" What an odd name to give your baby.

"My legal name is Ezra Armstrong, but everyone calls me Fang." He leans forward and kisses me on the forehead. "I'll call you in half an hour."

"Okay." I'm swooning so hard right now.

"Hey, if that dipshit," he nods in the direction Billy left, "tries to start something, call me."

"I will."

CHAPTER SIX

Fang

My head is still reeling from the events that took place earlier with Winter and her loser of an ex. I swear to all that is holy, if that man ever tries to mess with her again, I'm going to lay him out. He will be so jacked up that he won't be able to leave his bed for a month.

Sinner comes strutting toward me in his ridiculous cowboy outfit. My uncle is rough around the edges and is anything but a cowboy. I guess that's why it's called a costume, because we can dress as things we are not.

"Fang, I hear you're bookin' it early tonight." One thing about Sinner, he doesn't beat around the bush. He is straightforward. Guess that's where I get it from.

"You heard right." Technically, we are supposed to stay

until close, which is two in the morning. Before I met Winter, I was prepared to man my post. Now, I have other plans, and my uncle will just have to see reason because this is one thing I refuse to budge on. "I have a date to celebrate Winter's birthday."

Sinner's brows furrow. "Winter's birthday? Kid, winter isn't here yet. It's fall."

"Not winter as in the season." I laugh. "Winter is a girl I met and today is her birthday."

My uncle blows out a low whistle. "Fang going out with a girl?"

I can see that he is on the verge of shouting this to our brothers standing in hearing range. "Please don't make this a big deal." It's not like Winter and I are dating. I'm just doing her a solid since she's having the worst birthday. "We're not an item. Today's been shit for her, so I'm taking her out for her birthday."

Sinner scratches his beard. "Alright. I'll take your post." He slaps me on the back. "We're far enough into the night that there's no need to have me at the gate." Then, with all seriousness. "Don't think you won't get extra chores for ditching your brothers tonight."

I nod. Sinner is fair. He'll show grace where needed, but that man will also crack the whip to keep the club running smoothly. "Yes, sir."

Nodding back, Prez slaps me on the back. "Now, get outta here before I put you back to work."

On my way to the small trailer where the costumes are housed, I pass Ramon. My brother is lip-locked with a brunette. The line is smaller than it was at the beginning of

brother was gone, our attraction toward one another died. We're still friendly. After all, her father is a member of the Iron Devils.

Sandra extends her hand. "Hey, Winter, so good to meet you."

Winter shakes her hand. "Good to meet you." We follow Sandra to a table in the back corner. A usual for any member of the Iron Devils. "So, how do you know Fang?"

The smile that takes over Sandra's face is filled with sorrow. Both of us miss Vile fiercely. "Well, my father is a member of the Iron Devils."

"Iron Devils?" Winter looks at me then back at Sandra.

"It's the motorcycle club I'm in." I figured that since Winter attended our Halloween shindig tonight that she knew who we were. Looks like I was wrong about that.

"Oh." She smiles bashfully. "Sorry, I knew you were in a club, just didn't know the name."

"Phoenix is the Iron Devils' territory," I explain.

Winter nods, but I can tell this is going right over her head. That's okay, I don't expect everyone to have a complete understanding of club life. Sandra hands us our menus. "Mick, the owner of this diner, is my father. So, Fang and I go way back." The bell above the door rings, and Sandra glances over. "I'll be right back to take your order."

It doesn't take long for her to return. We order two Cokes and two stacks of pancakes. Mine with bananas and Winter's with blueberries. Before Sandra turns to leave, I add, "And make sure the cook adds *Happy Birthday* to Winter's stack."

Sandra nods. "Sure thing." Turning to Winter, she says, "Happy birthday."

Winter smiles. "Thanks."

"So, that loser dumped you on your birthday?" I'm not sure she wants to talk about her ex right now, but I just can't wrap my head around the fact he tossed her away so easily. I mean, damn, the other girl he was with doesn't hold a candle to the beautiful woman sitting in front of me.

"Yeah, by text." She crinkles her nose. "But let's not talk about Billy. I would hate to taint this evening with mention of that bastard."

Taking her advice, I change the subject. "So, is Winter your legal name, or a nickname?"

"Oh boy. I get asked that every time I meet someone." She laughs. "Winter is my legal name." Rolling her eyes, she says, "My mom had jokes the day I was born. She named me Winter Mynt Green."

"No shit?" I laugh. Damn, I bet she got picked on in school. What a terrible thing for a parent to do to their child.

Our food arrives, and Sandra, the cook, and the other waitress all join in on singing Happy Birthday to Winter. When other customers join in, Winter's face reddens in embarrassment. Once the celebratory song ends, we're left to ourselves.

"Fang." Winter bites her bottom lip, staring at the plate in front of her. "You didn't have to do this."

"Like hell I didn't." I was not about to let this heartbroken woman slip away without a proper birthday dinner.

"I mean, we've known each other for a couple of hours."

"True, we don't know one another." And normally, I wouldn't bother. I haven't been interested in a woman since I lost my brother, and Sandra and I lost interest in one another.

"Let's just say that your kisses earned my interest." She tries to hide a smile behind her glass, but I see it. "Besides, a girl like you deserves to be celebrated on her birthday."

Winter picks up her fork, spearing a piece of the blueberry stack. "Well, thank you." I nod since my mouth is full. "How long have you been in the club?"

Taking a drink to wash down the cake, I lean back. "I grew up in the club, but I patched in about five years ago."

Pausing with her fork midway to her mouth, she lifts a brow. "What does that mean?"

A lock of hair falls in her face and I reach over and tuck it behind her ear. "It just means that I'm an official member of the club."

"Oh." Blowing out a breath, she laughs nervously. "Sorry, I don't know anything about motorcycle clubs. Jelly's the one that enjoys that kind of thing."

"Nothing to be sorry for." I stab a banana off my stack and shove it in my mouth. "Someday, maybe I can give you the rundown. For now, I'll just say that before being patched in, one becomes a prospect. They must prove themselves trustworthy of the patch. The club and your brothers come first. You have to be willing to protect them at all costs."

Eyes wide, she sets down her fork. "That sounds kind of scary."

"It's a different world than yours, I'm sure, but it's one I'm proud to be a part of."

She tilts her head, studying me for a moment. "How long were you a prospect before you became a member?"

It thrills me to see her taking an interest in my life. I'm so used to the damn club bunnies that hang out at the compound. Those women are not interested in anything but sex. With them, the more the merrier. That used to be something that I enjoyed, but I've lost my appetite for those kinds of women. "A year and a half."

"Wow, that's a long time." Curiosity shines in her hazel eyes. "What made you want to join?"

"Easy, my father was the president when I was a kid, so I literally grew up inside the club. After he passed away, my uncle took his place." I don't want to scare her with the dangers that come with this lifestyle, so I leave out the fact that my father died in a shootout. Much like my brother. To this day, I feel guilty for not being able to save Vile from the bullet that landed in his chest. "The Iron Devils have always been my family."

The Iron Devils are my sanity.

My home.

The law of the club is the only life I've ever known. It's not a life I'm willing to give up.

CHAPTER SEVEN

Winter

Fang and I had an instant connection. I felt it at the haunted house before I ever knew his name. After my birthday pancakes, Fang drives us back to the carnival, where things are still in full swing.

How long do they plan on keeping this place open? It's almost midnight, and people are still dancing and drinking. Every ride still has a massive line. Vibration from my skirt pocket has me reaching for my cell phone.

It's a text from Jelly. One of many, I see.

JELLY:

Where are you?

JELLY:

You were supposed to text me to let me
know you made it safe.

JELLY:

OMG, Win, where the hell are you?

JELLY:

Is he being nice?

JELLY:

Is Mr. Iron Devil giving you orgasms at
least?

JELLY:

Ugh. You better text me back. Hell, I'd be
happy with a thumbs up. Anything.

Jeez, this woman is relentless. On a positive note, I know
she loves me. While Fang gathers a blanket from the trailer, I
type a quick message to my bestie.

We went to Mick's diner, like he mentioned
before we left. Highly recommend. Can't
believe I've never heard of it.

We're back at the carnival.

JELLY:

Where?

We're on our way to the lawn. They're
playing horror movies from midnight to two.

Fang slips his hand in mine and guides me toward the
lawn. We are passing the food court when a scream sounds.
At first, I think nothing of it. I mean, we're at a Halloween
carnival. People are drunk and having a blast on the rides. It's

been a loud night thus far. Even I let out a scream when walking through the haunted house earlier.

It's not until I hear a gunshot that I start to freak. My heartrate accelerates and beads of sweat dot my forehead. I immediately stop in my tracks. Fang does as well. His grip on my hand tightens, and he yanks me behind him.

Dropping the blanket, he drags me behind one of the food trucks. The door to the truck swings open and a shirtless man with Spiderman pants rushes out with a gun drawn. I gasp at the sight of the gun. Is he the one who fired the gun seconds ago?

Fang slaps a hand over my mouth. "It's okay, that's Haze. He's one of us."

Haze briefly gazes in our direction, then runs off toward the ruckus. Fang pushes me into the food truck. Immediately, he starts closing the windows and locking them in place. A second gunshot rings in the air, and I feel a panic attack coming on. "Fang?"

"Stay down," he says. Reaching behind him, he pulls out a gun. Did he have that on him while we were at the diner? He moves some boxes out of the way and motions for me to crawl under the counter.

Crouching down, my heart punches against my ribs with worry for Jelly. My best friend is wandering around out there with no one to save her. "Is this really happening?"

"Yeah, babe, it's really happening." Handing me his gun, he asks, "Can you shoot?" Holding the gun with trembling hands, I shake my head. I've never touched a gun in my life. "Okay." He positions the gun in my hand. "If anyone breaks in here, aim and pull the trigger."

"I don't think I can."

"Your life is in danger." He pulls open a drawer and retrieves a second gun, checking the magazine. I think it's called a magazine. All I know is he is checking the bullets. "Keep your finger off the trigger until you're ready to fire. I have to go help my brothers. Shoot anyone who breaks in, but please hold your fire if they use a key."

I nod. I wouldn't want to kill any member of his club. Not without reason. "My friend?"

"I will do what I can to find her." He starts shoving boxes in front of me to conceal my whereabouts. "In the meantime, I need you to stay put."

Outside, I hear scattering footsteps and more screaming as people seek cover. Fang places the last box in front of me, then I hear the door close. There's another shot. It's further away. I wish Fang were here to hold me. To protect me. But I know he needs to be out there to diffuse the situation. God only knows how many casualties there have been so far.

"Fang?" I cry out, but he's gone. Vanished into the chaos. More gunshots ring in the air, and I sob as quietly as I can. The last thing I want is to alert the shooter to my whereabouts. My phone buzzes and I slip it free to read the text.

JELLY:

Win, where are you? It's chaos out here.
There's a whole gang out here shooting at
the members of the Iron Devils.

Carnival music still filters through the speakers, eerie and adding to my rising panic.

A whole gang shooting at the Iron Devils? Oh, God. Fang.

He's running into danger. Of course, he went running into danger before knowing it was a gang shooting at his club members.

A breath catches in my throat, and a tear slides down my cheek. All I can hear is the beating of my own heart and the faint sound of the eerie Halloween track playing through the carnival speakers.

Another gunshot. This one is closer. I grip the gun tighter, praying I won't need to use it.

Instinct is telling me to run out that door and find Jelly. Find Fang. Instead, I stay hidden under the counter, frozen in place. The muscles in my legs start to cramp from being bent in an odd angle.

Buzz. Buzz.

JELLY:

Win, are you okay?

It's hard to type with trembling hands, but I get a reply in.

I'm okay.

I almost tell her where I am, but what if it's one of those gang members and not Jelly texting me? There's no way I'm giving out my location to a complete stranger. So, I call her. It rings twice before she answers. "Oh, thank God you're safe."

"Jelly, where are you?" I need to know she's safely hidden from the madness.

Her voice is shaky, much like I imagine mine is. "I'm near the Ferris Wheel, hidden behind the control booth."

"Can you see what's happening?" I need to know that Fang is okay.

"Sort of." She pauses when three more gunshots fire. "All the activity seems to be happening at the haunted house."

I wish more than anything that I could go back in time and start this day over. There's so much I would do differently, like never having come to this damn carnival. No, wait, that's a lie. I would not have had the chance to meet Fang if I hadn't come.

"Win, where are you?" My friend sounds tired and scared.

"I'm in a food truck, don't worry about me."

This night is one I will never forget. That's for sure. Maybe I can use details from this nightmare in my next novel. Thus far, the books I've written have been sappy love stories. There's been no horrific drama like that of tonight.

Footsteps hit the pavement outside. Heavy and growing closer to the truck I'm in. I end the call without a word and grip the gun with both hands. Waiting. Listening. The door rattles and I aim the weapon, my finger hovering near the trigger.

Thump, thump. Thump, thump. Thump, thump.

My heart pounds against my ribcage. Will I have the courage to pull the trigger? Tears blur my vision, and I blink them away. Then I hear it. A key. Fang said if they have a key, then it's one of his brothers and I'm safe. What if it's not one of his brothers? One of those gang members could have stolen the key.

The lock disengages and I hold my breath. Above the pounding of my heart, I hear the door swinging open. My finger never moves. I'm ready to shoot if necessary. When the box in front of me moves, I straighten my arms and aim, my shaky finger hovering over the trigger.

"Jesus," his familiar voice whispers. "Don't shoot."

"Fang." I drop the gun and push myself off the floor and into his arms. He catches me with ease. When I squeeze him tight, he grunts. Pulling back, I inspect him from head-to-toe. There, just above his collarbone, is blood. "Oh, my god, you're hurt."

"I'm okay." He presses my head back to his chest and caresses my hair.

I try to resist, but his hold on me is strong. "We need to get you to the hospital."

"No, I'll have our doctor look me over when I get back to the clubhouse." Fang kisses the top of my head. "Have you heard from your friend?"

"Yes, Jelly's safe. She's by the Ferris Wheel." Since the shooting has ceased, I'm assuming the fight is over. "How are your brothers?"

"Ramon took a bullet to the leg, but he's alive. Sinner's got Zero and Haze covering the south side. We took out most of them and the rest scattered like roaches when they saw they were losing." He takes a deep breath. "But I can guarantee you, this isn't over. Not by a long shot."

He sounds like he knows who is behind tonight's threat. "Fang, do you know who those people were?"

There's silence and I'm almost afraid of the answer. "They're the Hollow Bones."

"Hollow Bones?"

"They're a rival MC." He pauses, pulling back to look into

my eyes. Torment darkens his brown pools to black. "They are responsible for the death of my father and my brother."

Oh god. This poor man has lost so much. It makes my own heartache seem like a walk in the park. Now I feel foolish for dumping my problems with Billy on his shoulders. I don't know how long ago their deaths were, but it's clear it still haunts him.

CHAPTER EIGHT

Fang

Approaching footsteps have me shoving Winter behind me and drawing my weapon. We saw all the Hollow Bones flee, but you never know. One of them bastards could have hidden until finding the right time to come hunt us down.

"Yo, it's me." Zero waves a hand in front of the open door before stepping into view.

I relax and tuck the gun in the back of my pants. "How's it looking out there?" My sole focus was on getting back to Winter and making sure she was okay after we ran off the remaining Hollow Bones. Selfishly, I left my brothers to deal with sweeping the area and cleaning up the bodies.

"The area is secure. As for the bodies, they're loaded in the van and ready to be hauled to the dump." The dump is not like a trash dump. Well, it is but it isn't. It's a farm on the outskirts of town where we dump bodies off in the pig pens. Those hogs go crazy over fresh meat. "Oh, I have someone for ya."

Raising a brow, I ask, "Someone for me?" If it were one of my brothers, there would be no need for announcing they were here to see me.

Without saying another word, Zero moves aside, and a dark-haired woman rushes into the food truck. I recognize her from earlier. It's Winter's friend. Jelly, I think her name is. "Win?"

At the sound of her friend's voice, Winter releases my cut, where she had a death grip on the leather, and steps around me. "Jelly. Oh, thank God you're alive. I was so worried about you." She throws her arms around her friend.

While the two of them have their moment, I step out of the food truck to talk to Zero. Though I never leave her line of sight. I can't. The thought of something happening to her rips at my heart. It's a protectiveness I haven't felt since Vile.

"We need to get back to the clubhouse. Sinner is calling church." Zero looks behind me where the girls are chatting quietly. "What are your plans with her?"

"Her name is Winter." Gazing over at the food truck, I catch her staring at me. Nodding, I smile at her and turn back to my brother. "She's coming with me. Jelly too, I suspect." It doesn't look like Winter is going anywhere without her friend, and I can't say I blame her.

"I'll let Sinner know." Zero pulls his cell phone free, dialing my uncle as he waltzes off into the night.

Local law enforcement, friends of ours, have tended to the

civilians we had in attendance tonight. Outside of two casualties, our guests escaped unharmed. Thank the good Lord we have a few cops on our side. Otherwise, we'd be coming up with bail money.

Winter rushes to me the minute Zero is out of sight. She's careful of my gunshot wound. "Listen, I want you to come back to the clubhouse with me." I feel her stiffen in my arms. "Your friend is more than welcome to tag along."

At those words, Jelly exits the truck and places her hand on Winter's shoulder. "Honestly, Win, I think it's a great idea." Her gaze meets mine. "Besides, who better to protect us than the Iron Devils?"

"Perfect." I shoot off a text to Zero.

> Round up one of our guys to give Jelly a ride to the clubhouse. She's in no shape to drive, and I'm not about to let Winter out of my sight.

ZERO:
> Give me five minutes and I'll take her myself.

"Zero's coming back to give you a ride."

Jelly shakes her head. "That's not necessary, I have my car. We'll follow you."

Kissing the top of Winter's head, because I can't seem to help myself when it comes to her, I give a head shake of my own. "Absolutely not. This girl is not leaving my sight, and you are in no shape to drive." She opens her mouth to protest, but I speak over her. "It's non-negotiable. Zero will give you a ride, and one of our people will drive your car to the compound."

Jelly rolls her eyes. "Damn, you're bossy."

The bike roars through town. Pumpkins littering yards. Ghosts, witches, and bats hanging from the trees. People have long been in bed, most likely sleeping from a sugar crash. Winter clings to me like her life is on the line. It was, only an hour ago. Since we mounted my bike, she hasn't said a word. I'm sure she's processing everything I told her about the Hollow Bones and my father and brother.

We turn off on a dirt road a mile long. There are no houses out here—well, there's one, but it's abandoned. All of this is our land. Most of this land is wooded, and we use it to hunt. Mostly animals, but occasionally we do hunt people. Never an innocent. No, if we hunt a person, it's because they are a threat. Not just to us but to society.

Up ahead is our compound, concrete walls surround our premises. As we pull up to the large iron gate, Dawg and Ruffas—our prospects—are standing guard with rifles in hand. They set their weapons to the side and open the gates to let us through.

Dim porch lights cast shadows across the yard. I park my bike in line with the others, off to the side of the building. A few of my brothers stand on the porch with cigarette smoke curling amongst them. Blood coating their bodies.

I help Winter with the helmet, sliding it over the handlebars. Her eyes widen as she takes in the clubhouse. Large with dark stone siding. The Iron Devils emblem on the front door. Most of us have rooms here. Others have houses on the property.

Brushing a strand of hair from her face, I sling my arm over her shoulder. "Don't worry, you're safe here."

A bike roars through the gate, and we both glance back to see Zero riding in with Jelly sitting behind him. When she dismounts, she takes in the scene much like Winter did. As she approaches the building, she wrinkles her nose. "God, it smells like an ashtray out here."

Winter and I laugh.

Entering the house, Haze stands from the barstool he was perched on. Red stains his chest and I give him a once-over, looking for injuries. Lifting the bloody rag, he says, "Just a broken nose, most of this blood isn't even mine." Eyeing Winter, he crosses his arms. "Is this the birthday girl?"

Winter jerks in surprise. "How did you know?"

"Sweetheart," Haze gives her a genuine smile. A rare occurrence for him. "You were the talk of the carnival tonight." Nudging my shoulder, he continues. "This man here hasn't taken an interest in a woman in two years."

"Two years?" Winter questions, gazing at me with an expression I can't quite decipher.

Ramon is lying on the couch, blood oozing from the hole in his thigh. The doctor is administering medicine through an IV, and the nurse is getting items spread on a stainless-steel tray so he can tend to Ramon's wound.

Sinner whistles and silence ensues. "Church, now."

Winter grabs hold of my cut, pressing her body closer to mine. "Hey." I pinch her chin, tilting her head up so our gazes lock. "You're okay. You're safe here." Pointing to the door on the far-left side of the room, where Sinner disappears through, I say, "I'll be in that room."

Jelly takes Winter by the hand. "Come on, we can sit at the bar and drink Rum and Coke."

Winter doesn't let go, so I gently pry her fingers from my leather. "It's okay. Go have a drink. I'll be back as soon as I can. Sinner has called a meeting, and I need to attend."

Reluctantly, she releases me and follows her friend to the bar. Buzzcut nods at me, acknowledging that they are with me and he'll take care of them in my absence. When I enter church, I take in my brothers. Everyone is covered in blood. Some are worse than others. It's now that the pain of my own gunshot wound registers. Now that the adrenaline has worn off.

"Tonight was personal." Sinner scrubs his hands down his face. "The Hollow Bones have had it out for us since day one. You all know they're responsible for my brother's death, as well as my nephew's."

Everyone around the table nods. The younger members didn't know my father, but they did know my brother, Justin. AKA, Vile. "What's our plan of action, Prez?" I need to get a plan in action and seek retribution.

Pointing to my wound, Sinner says, "First, we take care of our injuries. I'll have Haze, Wolf, and Zero scope out the Hollow Bones. Have them gather intel and layout. It's time we take care of those bastards."

"Agreed." I fold my hands in front of me. It's time they get what they deserve.

Sinner dismisses us, and I can't exit this room fast enough. Winter is sitting on a barstool, sipping a glass of what I assume is Rum and Coke. The instant she sees me, she pushes the glass away and hops off the stool. "Thank God, I was going stir-crazy waiting on you."

Before I can wrap my arms around her, the doctor comes over with a kit, the nurse trailing behind him. "Time to get you looked at."

Haze drags a chair over for me to sit on. Winter holds my hand, and Zero takes Jelly up to the spare bedroom after she hugs Winter goodnight. Doc cleans my wound and busies himself with stitching me closed.

I can't tell you how grateful I am once he's finished. Now that there is no adrenaline running through my veins, exhaustion is setting in. A yawn stretches my mouth wide, and Winter traces the side of my face with a fingertip.

It's nice to feel a woman's touch. I didn't think I would ever desire this, to be honest.

"Okay, you're all set." Doc reaches into his bag and pulls out a bottle of pills. "Take these for the pain." He doesn't mention how frequently to take them. There's no need. With our lifestyle comes many injuries. Many that require the need for pain medicine. All of us are well aware of the dangers of these narcotics, and we're very cautious not to abuse them in any way.

Saying goodnight to the few brothers that are still lingering around, I guide Winter upstairs to my room. This woman has not let go of me for one minute. Not that I'm complaining. I'm not. It's nice to feel wanted. "You're safe here, Winter. I swear to you that no one will harm you. Not as long as I live and breathe."

Resting her head on my shoulder, she relaxes against me. "I believe you, Fang."

I need to fill her in on the dangers that lie ahead, but that will have to wait until morning. Right now, I'm beat. Emotionally and physically. With Jelly safe down the hall and Winter safe with me, all I want is to fall into bed and sleep.

CHAPTER NINE

Jelly and I sit at the bar nursing our spiked Coke. Tonight has been one nightmare I wish to forget. If I never hold another gun, it will be too soon. When the door opens and Fang walks out, I jump out of my seat and run toward him. It's strange, really, this feeling I have for Fang that I never felt for Billy.

I watch with a mix of fascination and horror as the doctor stitches Fang's wound. In the back of my mind, I take notes on the technique in case I decide to add this to a future novel. Does that make me sick and twisted? Possibly, but it will bring great detail to any book I decide to write that into.

The entire time the doctor is working on Fang, I caress his face. It's like he's a magnet. I'm drawn to him and have an urgent need to touch him in some form or fashion. "Okay, you're all set." Reaching in his black bag, the doctor pulls out a bottle of pills. "Take these for the pain." I notice he doesn't mention how many or how often to take them, and I wonder how many times these men have been in this same situation.

After the doctor packs up, Fang says goodnight to the remaining members in the room. Then he ushers me upstairs. Opening the door, I notice two things. First, his room is tidy. Second, it smells like him. A combination of cool spices, lavender, and musky wood. Taking a deep breath, I savor the scent that is Fang.

Cupping my face in his large hand, he says, "You're safe here, Winter. I swear to you that no one will harm you. Not as long as I live and breathe."

He says it with such conviction I can't help but believe him. Resting my head on his shoulder, I let him know just that. "I believe you, Fang." There is so much we need to discuss, but the events from tonight are catching up with me. Tomorrow we can talk about what happens from here.

When I wake, all is quiet. Not eerie, just the calm of the early morning. Like the world is taking refuge in the calm after the violent storm that shook our lives last night. Beside me, Fang snores softly.

With one arm bent behind his head and the other resting on his stomach, he almost looks angelic. Not like a bad boy biker, but beautiful and perfect. A man who loves hard and protects those in his inner circle.

How is it that I've known this man for less than twenty-four hours and he has already become my safe haven?

Slipping out of bed, I stretch my achy body. Padding across the cool wooden floor, I open the door and go in search of the bathroom. At the end of the hall is an open door, and thankfully, I can see a sink on the other side.

When I trek back to Fang's room, I wander over to the built-in bookshelf. Running my fingers across the perfect-bound books, I take stock of his reading interest. There is a good mix of thrillers, mysteries, and, to my utter surprise, romance.

Interesting.

On the edge of the shelf is a worn leather-bound journal. Curiosity gets the better of me, and I pick it up. It has creases on the cover from overuse. Opening the book and invading his privacy is not my intent, but my hands can't seem to stop themselves.

The first page has a name written on it.

Justin Lee Armstong

AKA—Vile

Beneath the name, in cursive handwriting:

I'm sorry I didn't protect you.

Oh no, I wonder if this is his brother. He did mention that the Willow Bones, no, it was Hollow Bones, had killed his brother. My chest tightens as I reread the name and his confession, over and over again. In that one line he wrote, I feel the weight of his world. His grief. If I could make this all better for him, I would in a heartbeat.

"Winter?" His voice startles me, and I nearly drop the journal.

My face heats with embarrassment. Embarrassed that I've been caught red-handed. Setting the journal back in its place, I spin around. Heart racing at having been caught snooping. Fang is lying on his side. His hand is reaching for the bottle of pain medicine. Those brown eyes of his veer to the bookshelf, then back to me.

"I'm sorry."

Popping the top off the bottle, he shakes out a pill and swallows it dry. "What are you sorry for?" Swinging his legs over the side of the bed, he stands. I can see the pain in his brown pools, but he never once winces. "Sorry for opening my journal and reading my private thoughts?"

I nod because I don't know what else to say.

Fang smiles, but it's sad. "My brother's name was Justin, but his club name was Vile. He was the better part of me. My twin."

"Twin?" I can picture him sitting around drinking beer and chatting with his brother. A man who shares his eyes and his smile.

"Yeah." He reaches out and strokes my cheek with the back of his fingers. "Identical."

Identical twins. He had a brother who looked exactly like him. I wonder if they sounded alike. Did they have the same hobbies? Well, outside of the motorcycle club. "Wow. Did you guys ever try to fool each other's girlfriend into thinking you were the other twin?"

Fang chuckles. "Actually, yeah."

"I bet the two of you were a mischievous pair."

"Oh, you have no idea." There's a pause. A sparkle in his eye. Maybe a fond memory. I stay silent and let him reminisce. He'll tell me when he's ready. "We gave our parents a run for their money, that's for sure." Sliding open the drawer on his bedside table, he pulls out a wooden picture frame.

"Vile was funny, loyal, and a fixer. If it was broken, he had to fix it. Bikes, cars, TVs, watches...even people."

After staring at the photo for a minute, he hands it to me. It's like looking at a picture of Fang mirrored side-by-side. Two identical men sit on the porch of what I recognize as the Iron Devils clubhouse, each with a beer in hand. "Fang, he looks just like you." I bring the photo closer for a better look. "Except he has a mole next to his eye."

Fang smiles. "Not many people notice that, even some of our friends that we grew up with couldn't tell us apart."

"Well, I'm an observer." It's part of what aids in my writing. "Can I ask about your brother?" He swallows, and I track the movement of his Adam's apple. After a moment, he nods. "I know you said the Hollow Bones were responsible for his death, but how?" I squeeze my eyes shut. "I'm sorry, I don't mean to pry. Apparently, I can't help being nosy."

"No, it's okay." Sitting down on the edge of the bed, he pats the spot next to him. Once I sit, he takes my hand and blows out a breath. "We, the Iron Devils, were riding through Dallas on our way to visit our Houston chapter." He takes the picture frame from me, tracing the photo within.

"Fang, I'm sorry." Placing my hand on his thigh, I give him a reassuring squeeze. "You don't have to talk about it."

Putting the frame back inside the drawer, he scrubs his hands down his face. "I want to." Haunted eyes stare back at me. "It's been two years, and you're the first person I want to share this with. Well, outside of the club...and Sandra."

Sandra? Makes me wonder about the relationship between those two. I make a mental note to ask about her another time.

"Dallas is the Hollow Bones' territory. We stopped at a diner on our way through and were ambushed on our way out." Those brown orbs glaze over, lost in a memory. "I was busy texting, so I was lagging behind. The first gunshot rang out, causing me to drop my phone and reach for my weapon. By the time I saw the glint of metal, they had already fired a second shot. The shot that killed my brother."

"Oh, my god." Scooting closer, I wrap my arm around him, offering comfort.

Leaning into my touch, he kisses the top of my head. Something I'm finding I like. A lot. "Yeah, by the time I reached his side, he was gone." There's a long pause. "Deep inside, I feel like I'm the one who killed my brother. I know it was the bullet of a Hollow Bones member, but I'm the one who was preoccupied with texting a woman instead of keeping my eyes peeled for danger. In our world, danger lurks around every corner. I should have been alert. Ready. I wasn't, and that's on me."

"No, that's on them. The Hollow Bones." I can't bear to see him torn up over an incident he isn't responsible for. "This is not your burden to bear."

"It's a burden I carry anyway."

I know what it's like to lose someone, but not this tragically. This is a loss I'm not sure I would wish on my worst enemy. Especially to witness the violent loss of your twin. A piece of your soul. That's a pain I can't fathom.

After a long pause, he asks, "You ever lose someone?"

"Yeah, I have." Resting my head on his shoulder, I take comfort in our shared grief. "I lost my mom to ovarian cancer four years ago."

"Damn, that sucks."

"It does." Tracing the lines on his abdomen, I confess, "She's the one who encouraged me to follow my dreams and write."

"Wait, you're a writer?"

I chuckle. "Yeah, romance."

Scooting back, he arranges the pillows under his arm. His eye twitches as he lifts his injured arm, but he never gives any other outward appearance of pain. "When you say romance, are we talking smut or just good old-fashioned love stories?"

"Love stories." I bite my bottom lip. "I'm not sure I could write those sexy scenes." Hell, I blush just listening to Jelly talk about sex. "After last night, I think I have an opening for a new story."

Fang huffs a laugh. "Yeah?" I nod to answer his question. "I hope this new story involves a sexy as hell Biker that swoops in to save the beautiful girl from a terrible ex and a rival gang."

"Oh, absolutely." Reaching out, I trace his strong jawbone. "He'll be a sexy, strong hero that saves the girl from flying bullets."

He winks. "Sounds like a book I need to add to my collection."

Now that I know he enjoys reading romance, I will be sure to bring him some of my books. "You'll be the first to read it."

A smile stretches Fang's mouth wide. Resting his head against the headboard, he closes his eyes. Taking this opportunity, I trace the outline of the tattoo on his forearm. VILE takes up the entire length of his forearm in bold black letters.

Fang cracks an eye open and watches my finger with a hint of sorrow. I wonder if he will ever look at this tattoo and not feel guilt for his brother's death. The sound of my text notification echoes in the quiet room. Standing, I round the bed and snag my cell phone off the bedside table. "Oh, sheesh."

Sitting up, Fang notices the blush heating my cheeks. "What is it?" he asks with amusement.

"Um, it's just Jelly."

When I don't say anything further, he nudges me. "What about Jelly?" A smirk lifts his lips.

I glance away because I can't look at him and say it. "She's asking me about biker sex."

Lifting a brow, he asks, "She have a romp in the hay with one of the bikers?"

"No." I shake my head. "She's asking how many orgasms you've given me so far."

He laughs. "And what did you tell her?"

"Nothing. There is absolutely nothing to tell because we did not have sex."

Holding out his hand, he nods toward my cell phone. When I place it in his waiting palm, he types out a text.

> So many orgasms, I won't be able to
> function for a week.

It's a fib, but she doesn't know that.

There is no holding in the laughter that spills from my mouth. Jelly will have a heyday with that text. In fact, I bet she corners me the first chance she gets, demanding all the details from my night with Fang.

No doubt she'll be disappointed in the truth.

CHAPTER TEN

Fang

The sound of Winter's laughter is the best thing I've heard in what feels like a lifetime. It's warm, real, and reaches down to my very soul. A place that has felt empty for the last two years.

It's like she belongs here, with me. Like she was made for me. Her presence is mending old wounds and healing that part of me that died with Vile. I've never been a fan of insta-love romance novels because that shit always seemed fake as hell. But as I watch her laughing at Jelly's response, I can't help but feel like this girl is my home.

Her phone has been pinging nonstop since I sent that text. I don't need to read it to know that her friend is pushing for details. Girls always seem to gravitate toward gossip. Especially where sex is involved.

Jelly might be sorely disappointed when she learns that Winter and I did nothing more than sleep and share our tragic pasts.

"Winter?"

She silences her cell phone and sets it aside. "Yes?" Her left eyebrow lifts when she sees the seriousness on my face. "Is everything okay?"

I cup her cheek, needing to touch her. "This isn't a one-night thing. You and I have something, a connection."

"Yeah, I feel it too." She leans forward, pressing her lips to mine. Unlike last night when she was putting on a show for her ex, this kiss is tender and full of promise. Promise for what, I'm not sure. I'm just ecstatic that she's willing to give this a shot.

A rap on the door, followed by Zero's voice, interrupts our moment. "Hang tight, babe." When I slip out of bed, there's a twinge in my shoulder. This isn't my first gunshot wound, most likely won't be my last.

I can feel Winter's eyes on me. Feel her concern. When I swing the door open, Zero is on the other side, wearing a scowl. "What's up?"

"They sent us a message." Tossing his phone to me, he says, "Those bastards blew up Mick's Diner."

All the blood drains from my face, and I feel lightheaded. "Mick and Sandra?"

Zero is quiet for a moment, which sets my nerves on fire. If anything happened to them, I'm not sure my sanity would be able to handle it. "They're fine." Knowing they're okay, I scroll through the pictures on his cell as he continues. "Mick has some scrapes, and Sandra had left for the night."

So much for us having time to get a plan in action. These assholes are thirsty for war, and I'm more than happy to give them just what they deserve. "Does Sinner know?" Of course, he knows. He's the president of this damn club. He knows everything that goes on in our world.

Zero nods. "Yep, he's called church."

"Be down in five." He doesn't say a word, just treks down the hall. As I shut the door, Winter hops off the bed, closing the distance between us. "What does this mean?"

Pushing her hair back, I kiss her forehead. "It means that things have escalated, and we need to act fast." I wish more than anything I could stay here. With her. We haven't had enough time to really get to know one another. There's no doubt in my mind that Sinner will send us off tonight to fight. To seek revenge. Not just for last night, but for my father and my brother.

Downstairs, it's eerily quiet. Everyone except Buzzcut and the prospects is in church. Waiting for me. Inside, Ramon is sitting off to the side with his foot propped up on a chair. Everyone else is in their assigned seat at the oval table.

Closing the door behind me, I take my place to the left of my uncle. Sinner releases a breath. "Last night, Mick's Diner was attacked. Luckily, Sandra had already left for the night, so she wasn't in danger."

"How is Mick?" Ramon asks.

"A little banged up, but not bad." Sinner steeples his fingers. "He did catch a glimpse of one of the Hollow Bones members."

Silence ensues as we wait with bated breath. The way Sinner mentions this member sounds like we might know who he is. "Who was it?" Haze asks.

Sinner rests his chin on his fingertips, eyes scanning the lot of us. The suspense is thickening, every one of us inching forward in our seats. "Ghost."

There's a round of gasps as we digest what we've just been told. Ghost used to be one of us. In fact, he was the enforcer when my father was president. I'm not sure what happened between the two, but my father and Ghost had a falling out when I was just a boy. Then my uncle became the president, and Ghost just disappeared.

Now, the man I viewed as an uncle when I was a kid is the man responsible for the bullet hole in my shoulder. Responsible for the attack on our Halloween Carnival and the attack on Mick's Diner.

And now that man is going to pay.

"As you all know, my plan to send Haze, Wolf, and Zero to scope out the Hollow Bones has been foiled. They attacked twice in one night, and I cannot in good conscious allow them the opportunity to strike again. We need to gear up and head out."

There is a sound of agreement throughout the room. Every member is ready for retaliation. We don't take threats lightly. Attack us and we strike back. We're the Iron Devils, and we rule with an iron fist.

Haze leans forward, his blue eyes glinting with the need for violence. "When do we leave?"

Sinner stands, "Sixteen hundred hours." Meaning four o'clock in the afternoon. That's only three hours away. Not enough time to pack and say goodbye to Winter. Winter, a girl I met less than twenty-four hours ago. A girl who has quickly wormed her way into my heart. My heart, the very thing that has been dead for way too long.

The minute the gavel slams, dismissing church, I'm up and out of the room in lightning speed. This is the moment I have been waiting for since the day Vile died. For two years, I have waited for Sinner to give the go-ahead for war. To seek revenge.

What has taken so long, you ask. Well, our Prez, my uncle, has been planning a strategy for so long. Waiting for the right time. Since the Hollow Bones president claimed not to have known the death of my father or the death of my brother, Sinner didn't think an attack on the whole club would be justified. Not to mention, it would break code and put us on every other club's shit list.

Like the good soldier I am, I go with my brothers to load weapons in our van. Not only are we strapping ourselves down with guns, knives, and extra ammo, but we are loading up extras in case we need them. We have no idea what exactly we are walking into.

Ramon hobbles out to our warehouse, a grimace on his face. He ignores the looks everyone shoots his way and starts strapping up. I know he wants to go with us. It's in his nature. It's our code to protect this club and our members at all costs, but Ramon is in no shape to help. Sure, he's the club's enforcer, but he isn't invincible. Regardless of what he may believe.

"Ramon." I shake my head. "You are in no shape to fight, man."

"The hell I ain't." Shouldering past me, he takes several boxes of ammo. Tossing multiple magazines on a stack of boxes, he loads each one of them, then slips them on his belt for later use. "Y'all ain't runnin' into danger without me." Squaring up, the look in his eyes is one of anger. Not toward me, but anger at the events that recently transpired. "I may be slow, but I ain't dead."

With that, he pops a pain pill, spins on his heel, and treks back the way he came. I'll leave that for Sinner to deal with, knowing my uncle, and club life, Ramon is going with us. No matter our injuries, if we are up for the fight, we fight.

Taking the stairs two at a time, I ignore the throb building in my shoulder. My only thoughts are getting up to my room to say goodbye to my girl. *When the hell did I start to think of Winter as my girl?*

Opening the door, I find Jelly sitting on the edge of the bed. She and Winter are leaning against each other like they need the other to survive. When my boots thump on the hardwood, Winter's gaze lifts to mine. In the two hours I've been gone, dark circles have formed under her eyes. It's like she feels the gravity of this situation. A situation that doesn't involve her. Other than what she was in the midst of last night.

Untangling from her friend, Winter leaps off the bed and rushes toward me. "Y'all are leaving." She's not asking, she knows.

"Yeah," I whisper into her hair. Hair that smells like citrus and musk. "We ride out at four." How does my heart ache more for this woman I barely know than it ever did for Sandra?

Winter's arms tighten around me. "Promise me you'll be back." I don't promise to be back. We are marching into battle. There's no promise of making it through the night unscathed. My silence says it all. Body trembling, she presses closer like she's trying to embed herself into my body. "Fang, promise me you'll be back."

"Babe, you know I can't." Nodding, she jumps into my arms. Biting the inside of my cheek to keep from grunting in pain, I carry her to the bed. Jelly quietly exits the room, giving us time alone. Thank God. Don't get me wrong, I'm glad Winter has Jelly to lean on, but this is my time. Jelly will get her back in an hour when we ride out.

Leaning back, she gazes down at the bandage peeking out from under my cut. "Your shoulder."

"Don't worry about that." I cup her face and lean forward. Pressing my lips to hers. "We're not going to worry about my injury or what ifs." Tears fill her eyes. "What we are going to do is make this a goodbye to remember. One that gives me purpose and helps me strive to return."

"You have to return to me." She runs her fingers through my messy hair. "I need you. As crazy as it sounds, I feel like I've known you my whole life, even though we barely know each other."

"I get it." I kiss her forehead. "The moment you kissed me in front of your ex, I knew you were meant to be mine. Our story isn't over before it's begun. Nah, you and I were meant to ride this crazy life together."

Keeping my gaze on hers, I lean forward, kissing her slowly and deeply. Needing to taste the one that has breathed life back into my sorry soul. Her hips rock against me like she can't get enough. Neither can I, but I don't want our first time to be rushed because I'm leaving for war with our rivals.

Gripping her hips, I halt her movements. "Not like this."

Lifting a brow, she says, "Not like what? Like you're going off and I may never see you again." She tries to push off me, but I hold her firmly in place. We are not doing this. Not having our first argument and then me watching her walk away mad, while I leave her behind. That was my parents, and I will not let that be us.

"Stop." I stand and drop her on the bed, then crawl over her. "We aren't doing this. We're not going to fight less than an hour before I leave."

Gazing up at me, she blinks, and the tears that have been building finally break free and trail down her face. "I'm sorry, I don't know what's wrong with me."

"Yeah, you do." I rest my weight on my forearms and lean down, my lips hovering over hers. "You have strong feelings for me and know that I'm riding into a scary as shit war." She nods. "But I don't want our first time together to be rushed, or because you fear you'll never see me again." Kissing her, I give her all I've got. Letting her know that I feel it too. The fear, the anxiety, the connection. "When we do have sex, I don't just want to devour you. I want to spend my time committing your body to memory. Worship you the way you were meant to be worshipped."

"Okay." She wraps her arms around my neck and kisses me. Her tongue invades my mouth, exploring. It's sweet, just like her. When I take charge, she yields. Winter is like a cool, sweet dessert in the middle of summer.

This girl is everything I never knew I needed. Now, I just need to ensure I make it home safe and sound.

CHAPTER ELEVEN

Winter

Fang and I lay tangled up in each other's arms until it's time for him to leave. I feel like a fool for crying over a man I don't know. Let's face it, I don't know him. Sure, I know his name, and I know about his father and brother. But I don't *know* him, and here I am shedding tears as I watch this man walk out the door.

I step out onto the porch and watch him mount his bike. His brown eyes find mine, and he winks before slipping the helmet over his head. Inside of me is a tornado wreaking havoc on my emotions.

Two men wearing leather vests open the gates. There is a revving of engines, then the Iron Devils file out of the gates in an orderly fashion. Trailing behind the motorcycles is a large white utility van. A van that I suspect is housing weapons, and who knows what else.

The gates close once the van passes through, and I continue to stand and listen to the roaring engines as they fade into the distance. I don't know how long I stand out on the porch, but when a hand slips into mine, I turn to see my best friend standing next to me. "Come on, let's get you something to eat."

Shaking my head, I tug free from her grasp. "I can't leave."

"Win." Jelly jams a thumb over her shoulder, aiming at the clubhouse. "There is nothing for us here. We need to return to town and resume our normal lives. You have a book to write, and I have a job that will harass me if I'm not back in the morning."

She's right. I know she is. Besides, I'm sure Buzzcut and those two at the gate don't want me in their space. Especially right now with everything going on with their rival. When Fang comes home, he'll call me.

"Fine, but only because I am on a tight deadline." I let her drag me inside and up the stairs. Every few steps I have to blink tears from my eyes. It doesn't make sense how fast this thing with Fang happened. How deeply my feelings for the man have grown.

Last night, when I approached him, it was only supposed to be a slap in the face of my ex. It was never supposed to go further than that. But that first kiss rocked me to my core. Then the way he protected me from flying bullets and cared for me like I was worth saving. That meant everything to me. He reached a part of me that hasn't been touched in what feels like ages.

When we reach Fang's room, Jelly releases my hand. Neither of us utters a word. She waits for me to open his bedroom door and enter before trekking down the hall to the other room to gather her belongings.

Stepping over the threshold, I breathe in deeply. The room smells like Fang. I miss him. Miss his touch. His kiss. God, this is torture. Walking over to the bed, I snatch up his pillow and bury my face in it. How am I supposed to go back to my mundane life and not be able to touch him? To smell him.

Decision made, I gather my cell phone, purse, and Fang's pillow. When I fling the door open, Jelly is standing on the other side. The moment her eyes land on the pillow in my arms, she lifts a brow. "Seriously? You're stealing his pillow?"

"Like you haven't stolen men's shirts in the past." That girl has gotten away with shirts, sweatpants, and jackets. The closet in her spare bedroom is full of clothes she has taken from past lovers. That would make her the pot, me the kettle.

Jelly rolls her eyes. "Fine, take the man's personal belongings."

Downstairs, Buzzcut is on the phone. At the sound of our descending footsteps, he turns around. "Hold on a sec." Glancing at the pillow in my arms, he crosses his arms over his chest. "What exactly do you think you're doing with that?"

"I, um." Well, I guess I didn't think of the repercussions of stealing Fang's belongings while his club brothers were in the house. Looks like this Buzzcut guy is about to hand me my ass. "You're scary as hell."

Why did I say that?

Jelly tugs on my shirt sleeve. A signal for me to shut up. Buzzcut, on the other hand, cracks up laughing. Putting the cell phone back to his ear, he says, "Yo, your chick thinks I'm scary as hell."

Your chick? Is he speaking to Fang?

"Chick was trying to leave with your damn pillow, like some lovestruck puppy." Whatever Fang says has Buzzcut in a fit of hysterics. Shaking his head, he hands me the cell phone, a splintering crack on the screen.

I've never been referred to as a lovestruck puppy. I'm not sure if I should be offended. Pressing the phone to my ear, I say, "Hello?"

"So, I hear you're trying to sneak off with my pillow?" Oh god, does he think I'm a nutcase? Is this going to be a deal-breaker with this man? I don't know the protocol when it comes to a romantic relationship with an MC member.

"I'm sorry, I'll put it back. It's just that it smelled like you, and I wasn't ready to give up that scent just yet." Now I'm rambling like an idiot. If he wasn't ready to get rid of me before, I'm sure he is now.

"No." There's laughter in his voice. "Take it with you."

"Seriously, you don't mind?" Relaxing my shoulders, I smile at Jelly, letting her know all is good.

"I don't mind." There are voices in the background, and he pulls the phone away to answer. "Hey, I hate to do this, but I need to speak with Buzzcut."

Any joy I had at hearing his voice is being drowned out by the sadness of having to say goodbye. Again. "Okay."

"I'll call you when I can." In the background is the roar of engines as they prepare to take off from wherever they stopped. To be honest, I'm scared to death of what Fang is about to do. For all I know, he's off to sign his death sentence. Rather than voice those fears, I decide to put on a brave face. The fact is, I'm highly attracted to the handsome biker, and apparently that comes with a side of danger.

"Talk to you then." I refuse to say goodbye. Right now, that seems so final, and this thing between us is far from over. It's just beginning, and I so desperately want to see where our journey takes us. Handing the phone back to Buzzcut, I wave and follow Jelly out of the clubhouse.

Before we can make it down the steps, a tall guy with broad shoulders steps in our path. Honestly, he looks like he could take down a grizzly bear one-handed. I don't remember seeing him last night, and I take a step back. For all I know, this could be one of the Hollow Bones that shot up the carnival last night.

A hand lands on my shoulder, bringing a startled yelp from me. "Chill, it's me." I turn around to see Buzzcut standing behind me. "Snake is going to escort you home." Snake? What is it with bikers and their crazy names? If things with Fang and me work out, they'd better not try to nickname me. They suck at names. Well, except for Fang. His name rather suits him.

Throwing my hands on my hips, I shake my head. "That's not necessary."

Buzzcut shrugs a shoulder. "The order came from Fang. If you want to leave, you'll be escorted home."

Jelly takes my hand. "Win, after last night, I say we let him follow us home. That way, he can keep an eye out for any rivals that might be lurking about." How is she so calm right now? This girl acts like it's just another day.

How the hell did I get myself mixed up in this chaos? Before yesterday, my life consisted of writing and Billy. My days were calm and relaxed. Well, except when Jelly occasionally drags me out to the club. Even then, it was nothing like this. Today I'm being escorted around and worrying about who might be watching me from the shadows.

Part of me wonders if pursuing Fang is worth the trouble his biker club brings, but the other part, the much bigger part, wants Fang and everything attached to him. Like I told him earlier, these events will make for great inspiration for the next book I write.

Not saying a word to Snake, I give Buzzcut one last glance and follow Jelly to her car. When she turns the ignition, I hug Fang's pillow and rest my head on the glass. My mind and body are so exhausted that I could sleep for a week.

Lose Yourself filters through the speakers, and I close my eyes, allowing the music to lull me to sleep. The darkness is inviting, and my body relaxes into the seat. In the background, I can hear Jelly, but my brain shuts out the outside noise, allowing me a few minutes of bliss.

Normally, I'm a light sleeper. Every little noise stirs me from slumber. Not this time. This is the hardest I've ever crashed in my life. When I open my eyes, it's to Jelly shaking me. "Thank god." She grabs her purse from the backseat. "I was afraid I'd have to sit out here all day and listen to you snore like a freight train."

It takes a minute for my brain to register what she just said. When her words sink in, my mouth drops open and I smack her arm. "Excuse me, I do not snore." My best friend has the audacity to roll her eyes and crack up laughing. How rude.

Unbuckling the seatbelt, I exit the vehicle and trail after Jelly. Seeing Snake walk out my front door causes me to pause at the front of Jelly's car. When did that man go inside my house? He was following along behind us. Glancing back, I see his bike parked behind Jelly's car. Then a thought occurs to me. How the hell did he even get into my house?

Before I can question him, he hands Jelly a set of keys. Her keys. That's when it registers that she must have given him her key so he could look the place over. Make sure that there weren't men inside waiting to kill us.

Just the thought of that causes butterflies to stir low in my belly, and not the good kind.

He says something to my friend, then comes toward me. Of all the Iron Devils I've met, Snake is the most unsettling. I would have much preferred Ramon or Ruffas to have escorted us home today. I suppose if Fang trusts this man, I should too.

Snake nods toward my garage. "I'm gonna park my bike in the garage so it's out of sight. I'll be sitting in the car to keep watch."

No asking, just telling. I swear, these men think that because they belong to some dangerous club that they can do whatever they want, whenever they want. "Just like that, you're going to come into my home and start barking orders?"

"Something like that." The garage door opens, and I realize that while I've been standing here listening to Snake, Jelly has gone inside and opened my garage door for this man.

Without another word, Snake walks around the car and starts moving his bike.

As he's getting his bike out of sight, an unsettling chill races up my spine, leaving icy trails in its wake. I rub the back of my neck and start looking around. Nothing appears to be out of the ordinary, yet I can't shake the feeling that I'm being watched.

Maybe it is a good idea that Snake will be hanging around. As much as he makes me nervous, this feeling is so much worse. Like a killer is lurking around the corner, waiting for the right time to put a bullet in my head.

CHAPTER TWELVE

Fang

Engines roar our war cry as we race through the streets. Sinner rides the head of the line. Wolf and I ride behind our president. Normally, it would be Wolf and Ramon since Wolf is the VP and Ramon is the enforcer. With Ramon's gunshot wound, he is riding in the Van at the end of our formation.

Gripping the handlebars in a death grip, I do my best to put her out of my mind. I cannot be distracted on this mission. Being distracted will end in my death, and most likely several of my brothers. They need me to be laser-focused. Not pining like a damn boy discovering puppy love.

Get your act together, Fang. Your family is depending on you.

The smell of gasoline and desert invades my senses. We're

entering neutral territory between Iron Devils and Hollow Bones. The space where our Prez has met with theirs. War is right at our fingertips. I'm sure they are on the lookout for us. They would be dumb not to be. You don't attack another club's territory and expect peace. That's not how this works.

Raven hair and bright orange highlights are all I see as I follow in line on these dirt roads. The softness of her lips when she kissed me. That come-get-me look as she pressed herself against me. Silently begging for me to take her. To claim her.

Gritting my teeth, I shove thoughts of her to the back of my mind and focus on the road ahead. I'm going to end up breaking that poor girl's heart. She doesn't belong in my world. Winter is sweet, pure, and innocent. I'm the exact opposite. My lifestyle is dangerous. It's nothing but leather, code, and blood.

Winter is the kind of woman who deserves a forever. All I can offer her is war and goodbyes.

When Sinner raises a fist, we slow and follow him to the edge of the woodlands. On his signal, we shut off our engines and silence our cell phones. The last thing we need is for our phones to go off while in the middle of sneaking up on the enemy.

Sinner dismounts his bike and pulls out a sheet of paper from the inside of his cut. Once the van pulls to a stop, Ramon hops out, tossing back a pain pill. Our Prez spreads the paper on the hood of the van. "I spoke with my intel guy. He says the Hollow Bones have a camp just on the outskirts of this buffer zone. I drew a map based on what I found on the internet. It's not much to go on, but there should be a warehouse northeast." He points in that direction. "And an old ghost town northwest."

I make a mental note of the hand-drawn map, the little markers, and the roads. "So, we don't have a location, just the general *out yonder somewhere?*" Sinner's intel guy is a crackhead with rotting teeth who is willing to do or say anything to get his next fix. I trust him about as much as I trust a rabid dog not to bite.

My uncle grunts. "If the intel is wrong, or we're ambushed, I'll be sure ol Jack gets what's comin' to him."

"Any chance Ghost is out there?" I'm jonesing to get my hands on that bastard. Make him pay for all he's done.

Sinner gives me a stern look. "If he is, we're taking him alive."

"But—"

"There are no buts." Sinner points a finger in my face. "I want answers. You need answers. He's coming with us alive." Then, slapping a hand on my shoulder, he nods toward the northwest. "Fang, I'm sending you to do what you were born to do."

Every member is silent as my uncle speaks. His word is law. We stand still and await our orders. For a long beat, Sinner stares at me. His eyes softening for a brief moment. He knows this could be the last time we see each other.

"Alright, everyone to my left goes with me. Everyone else will follow Fang's lead. Kill all the Hollow Bones except one. We need Ghost alive." There's a chorus of agreement from every member. Lastly, Sinner locks eyes with Ramon. "Ramon, you can hang back, keep a lookout from the van. No one expects you to go running out there with a freshly wounded leg."

Ramon shakes his head. We all know the answer. That man is loyal to a fault. There is no way in hell he will sit out on a war. "Appreciate it, Prez, but I'm good. I'm here to do my job."

"Good." Sinner motions for his crew to gather weapons. "You're with me."

"Sure thing." Ramon limps toward the back of the van to load up.

Dawg takes his place behind the wheel. It's his job as a prospect to stay and keep watch over our weapons and report in with any suspicious activity in the buffer zone. Wolf slings a rifle over his shoulder. "Let's get them bastards."

I nod. Wolf is a good man. As vice president, I fully expected Sinner to put him in charge of this crew. Knowing my uncle trusts me to lead this mission means the world to me. One day, in the distant future, I would love to run the club. This is a step in that direction.

Right as I'm getting ready to signal my team, I spot Ramon bracing himself on the side of the van. Sweat is starting to soak through his shirt, probably from the pain. "Hey, man, you good?"

Taking a deep breath, he nods. "Yeah, I'm good. Pain is a luxury none of us has time for."

Well, that is something I can respect.

Ramon pushes off the van and limps toward Sinner and his crew. Lifting my hand, I twirl my finger, signaling my team. As I walk northwest, they follow close on my heels. Each step we take is closer to revenge and justice. Now that we are heading toward the enemy, my body buzzes with energy. Like a livewire in my veins.

For fall weather, it's unnaturally hot today. Sweat drips onto my collar as we march across the desert floor. Nothing can be seen for miles. It's a good thing the Iron Devils have a daily workout routine to stay in shape. There's no telling how many miles we'll be walking to get to this camp. Not to mention, we have an all-out war once we get there. This life-style is not for the faint of heart.

Not a word is spoken. Each of us is focusing on what's to come. The severity of the situation hangs over our heads like a dark cloud. In the pit of my stomach, I feel it. This is the spot where the Hollow Bones are hiding out. I reach for my cell phone to shoot Sinner a text, but stop myself. What if my gut is wrong? Asking him to change course would then result in the enemy escaping unscathed.

"What is it?" Wolf asks, his eyes tracking the movement of my hand.

"I'm probably wrong." This is the first mission Sinner has allowed me to lead. I do not want to screw it up.

"Possibly." He shrugs a shoulder. "What is it?"

I'm not some newbie who thinks he knows it all, and I don't want to come across as such. Not that I think Wolf would see me as such if I voice my gut feeling. "I was going to shoot Sinner a text to change course." Pointing to my stom-ach, I say, "I feel it right here, the Hollow Bones are camping out in the ghost town."

Wolf nods. "Gut feelings are rarely wrong." Turning his gaze back to the path ahead of us, he says, "But good call on not contacting Sinner. Those fools could have split in two directions, anticipating our ambush."

That right there is the second reason behind my not texting my uncle. Because if it were us camping out, we would be expecting them to attack, and we would plan accordingly.

Wolf and I slow our steps at the same time. Out in the distance, I see the abandoned town. Like Sinner said, it's a shell of a town. A place where even ghosts refuse to go. We stick to the shadows of the woodlands. Our feet landing softly on the ground so as not to make noise. The last thing we need is to give away our arrival.

Coming up to the back of a building, I inch my way around the side to view the main road. Wolf is right behind me, and the others are following in line. As I peer around the corner, I see a bunch of buildings that are in sad shape. Several are missing windows, and most have doors barely hanging on the hinges.

The place looks deserted, with the exception of one building at the far end. El Camino Saloon. There is a faint glow flickering from within. I don't spot movement in any of the other buildings. Outside of El Camino, the place is a graveyard for a past life. Motioning for everyone to retreat, we make our way back toward the shelter of the trees to discuss our plan of action.

"What's the plan, Fang?" Wolf steps beside me with an inquisitive look.

Every eye is on me. Watching, waiting for instruction. "We stake the place out. Wolf, Dash, and Zeke, you take the east side of town. Rage and Hitch, you're with me. We'll cover the west side." Everyone nods, dividing accordingly.

"Come nightfall, we invade their camp. Tonight, we show no mercy."

Fists punch the air above, and we all open our mouths in a silent battle cry. The Iron Devils are ready to eliminate the threat and get justice for our fallen brothers. Victory is ours. I just pray it doesn't cost us the lives of our own.

Wolf leads his men east, leaving Rage and Hitch to follow me. We scope out the area, looking and listening for signs of life. All is quiet. Not a sound to be heard. Entering through a back window of a dilapidated building across from El Camino, the stench of dirt and rotted wood invades my senses. The dirt tickles the back of my throat, and it takes all I have to keep from coughing. I can tell by the redness of their faces that the guys are struggling as much as I am.

Crouching behind the window, I pull out a pair of binoculars so I can see what's happening across the road. At first, I don't see any movement. The only indication that the building is, or was, occupied is the kerosene lantern sitting on the bar top.

I'm just about to hand the binoculars to Hitch when a shadow flits on the wall. A second later, a scrawny redhead strolls into view. With a beer in hand, he perches on a ratty barstool that looks two seconds from crumbling to the ground. After a few beats, six others join him. Each man is sipping from a bottle. Seemingly unaware of our presence.

Damn, watching that makes me thirsty. Not necessarily for a beer, any cold beverage will do. I pass the binoculars to Hitch and tell the guys to stay and keep an eye on the Hollow Bones while I slip into another room to contact Sinner.

> We have activity out here. You?

It doesn't take long for him to reply.

SINNER:

> Nada. We've swept the entire area, and nothin.

> So far, no signs of Ghost. I counted seven men in an old saloon across the street.

As I'm waiting for Sinner's reply, a text from Wolf comes through.

WOLF:

> There are no signs of life out here on the east. Buildings are all void. One caved in as we were leaving.

Sounds like the Hollow Bones are all in El Camino. Either we are extremely lucky, or this is a trap. I send an update to Sinner.

> Wolf said there are no signs of the HB on the east side of the town. This could very well be a trap.

WOLF:

> I'm heading back. Ping me your location.

I do just that and give him instructions on where to enter to keep out of sight of the saloon. In the meantime, Sinner responds.

SINNER:

> That's a very real possibility. Stay on guard.
> We're heading your way.

Just like I did with Wolf, I give Sinner the rundown on where we are in relation to the saloon. The night is growing darker by the minute. Time to attack is vastly approaching, and personally, I cannot wait to kick some ass.

Tonight, I'm out for blood.

Tonight, we seek vengeance.

CHAPTER THIRTEEN

Winter

The hot water beating down on me is refreshing. Sure, I had a shower at Fang's, but standing in my own shower, resting my forearms on the tile wall, is heaven on earth. I can practically feel the tension melting off me.

Fang called me last night, after they arrived in El Paso. They got a room—well, several rooms—to get some rest before marching into the enemy's camp. I actually slept decently knowing that he was safe for the night. Now, I'm back to worrying.

Knock, knock.

The door creaks, and I peer through the glass of the shower door as Jelly saunters into the bathroom. "How're you doin?"

"Eh." That's all I say. I mean, what else is there to say? We got mixed up with a biker gang whose enemy shot up the Halloween Carnival the other night. Now we have a guard dog because we might be in danger.

Hopping onto the counter, Jelly taps on her cell phone, then tosses it to the side. "I made coffee."

Because that's what we need as the sun is going down. Stimulants to keep my mind awake so I can lie in bed all night worrying about things I have no control over. Maybe I'll stay up tonight and get some writing done. Anything to shift my focus from Fang and the Hollow Bones.

"Wanna stay up and watch some Swayze dance action?" This girl and her fascination with that old movie.

That's my Jelly-Bean, always taking care of me and keeping me grounded when I feel my life start to spiral out of control. No matter how big or small the circumstance, she is my rock. The one person who has never let me down.

Shutting off the water, I open the glass door, and Jelly tosses me a towel. "Hurry up, I'll pour the coffee and queue the movie."

Slipping into a tank top and silk shorts, I towel-dry my hair and pin it up in a clip. As promised, Jelly is sitting in the recliner with a cup of coffee in each hand. Taking one of the cups, I perch myself on the love seat and prop my feet on the coffee table.

Ten minutes into the movie, and my focus shifts to Fang. The coffee, though I drink every last drop, is bland and unfulfilling. I feel like a zombie wasting away over here. Every few minutes, I check my cell phone, hoping to find an update from Fang.

I need him to come back in one piece.

Because if he doesn't—

Well, I'm not sure my heart can handle a second heartbreak. Even if I've only known the man for a couple of days, mourning his absence would bring me to my knees. This has me thinking. Is insta-love real? Is it possible to fall in love at first sight? Because that's what this is starting to feel like.

Yes, I'm still hurt about what Billy did, but this thing with Fang is so much deeper than what I had with Billy. As crazy as that sounds.

"You're thinking too loud." Jelly must have noticed that I'm lost in my own world. Normally, she wouldn't take her eye from the screen, not when this movie is playing.

I nearly drop the empty coffee cup when she speaks. "Huh?"

"I can practically hear the gears turning in your head." She pauses the movie and moves to sit next to me. "He'll be back."

"You don't know that."

"No." Jelly takes the ceramic cup from my hands, placing it on the coffee table. "But you have to believe he will. Otherwise, you'll drive yourself crazy with worry." I know she's right, yet my stomach is all twisted up with worry for his safety.

Chewing on my thumbnail, a habit I haven't had since high school, I twist in my seat to face her. "You think I'm nuts, don't you?"

She shakes her head. "No, but you and him remind me of those cheesy love-at-first-sight romances." Crinkling her nose, she adds, "It's quite sickening, if you ask me." A smile spreads on her face. "I don't know the man, but he already is ten times the man Billy was, is, and will ever be."

We sit in silence, staring at the television. A first kiss frozen on screen. I'm not sure how long we sit there, her hand resting on my knee. It's not until the screen times out and goes black that I glance over at my best friend.

Jelly is starting to doze off. "Why don't you go to bed?" She shakes her head and sits up, but I wave her off. "Seriously, I'm just going to sit at my desk and get some words written. My editor has been hounding me for two weeks. My deadline is approaching and I'm four chapters behind."

"Fine." She stretches out on the couch, rather than heading off to the bedroom. "But I'm sleeping right here. That way I'm in earshot."

Rather than argue about the fact that she would get better rest in an actual bed, I nod and head off to my office. In the pit of my stomach, I feel that something isn't right. Is it Fang? Did he get hurt? Or worse.

As I fire up the computer, the hairs on the back of my neck stand on end. Crossing the room, I peer out the window. Snake is sitting on the curb across the street, a lit cigarette dangling from his lips.

As long as he's out there keeping watch, we're safe. Right?

Taking Snake's presence as a good sign, I sit at my desk and pull up the manuscript. Every tick of the wall clock echoes in my mind. Taunting me. Reminding me that life is moving forward.

For the umpteenth time, I pick up my cell phone. Still no word from Fang. Ugh, I hate this. The unknowing. Placing my fingers on the keyboard, I start typing, but nothing makes sense. I delete and then type some more. Delete. Type. Delete. Type. Delete.

"This is stupid." Shoving the offending keyboard away, I lean back and stare at the ceiling.

A floorboard creaks, sending chills down my spine. I freeze, holding my breath and praying that it's just Jelly. Though I know it isn't her, because my desk faces the office door and I never saw it open.

I should have listened to Fang when he insisted, I stay at the clubhouse. If we had stayed there, then we would be under the protection of the Iron Devils. The clubhouse is a fortress. No one gets in or out without permission.

My heart slams into my ribcage, beating fiercely. The breath I'm holding is burning my chest, and I release it, gulping in air. "Snake?" I whisper.

There's no answer. Surely, he would have shown himself by now. He knows the gravity of the situation. He wouldn't scare me like this. Knowing that Fang would have his hide for giving me such a fright.

"Snake?" I call out, my voice high-pitched. "Is that you?"

Silence. No reply. No footsteps.

Just a spine-chilling quietness that has me reaching for my cell phone. I bring up Fang's number but refrain from hitting call. He's on a mission and can't afford the distraction. Shutting the screen off, I tiptoe to the doorway to check on Jelly. She's still stretched out on the couch, sleeping.

Heading toward the kitchen, I snag a knife from the block. If someone is in my house, I'm not going down without a fight. "Jelly." When she doesn't stir, I call her name a little louder. "Jelly."

Startling, she rolls off the couch with a thud. "Ow." Glancing up at me, she frowns. "What?"

I lift a finger to my lips to indicate for her to remain quiet. Grabbing the cast-iron skillet from the stovetop, I inch my way toward her. "Which one?" I whisper. She takes the knife. "I heard someone in my office."

"Shit." She snags her cell phone off the coffee table, dialing a number. Faintly, I can hear Snake's voice through the phone pressed to her ear. "Someone's in here." Apparently, he ended the call because she pulls the device away, and the screen is black.

Next thing I know, the front door gets kicked in. The man had a key to my house, and rather than unlock the door, he kicks it in. I hope he knows I will bill him for the replacement. Men. I swear. "Where?"

With the skillet still in hand, I point toward my office. He marches in with guns drawn. Jelly and I stand arm-in-arm as we wait. Three seconds pass, then five. Still no shouting. No gunshots.

Nothing.

Mind reeling, I start to imagine Snake walking into that semi-dark office and one of the Hollow Bones slicing his throat from behind. Or a scenario much sinister. Snake secretly being a Hollow Bones member and working with a buddy. Could he be in there waiting for us to seek him out so he and his friend can capture us?

Oh hell no. I'm not waiting around to find out if he's truly the enemy.

Nudging Jelly, I motion toward the front door. "Let's get out of here."

A look of disbelief crosses her features. "What? Are you insane?"

Just as I open my mouth, Snake exits my office, holstering one of his weapons. "Grab your shoes, we're leaving."

"Did you find him?" Jelly asks.

He shakes his head. "Room is clean, but the side window is open." Turning toward me, he asks, "Did you open that?" I shake my head. Knowing that Fang felt we needed a babysitter, I never opened any windows. Besides, late at night, I like to keep them closed. You never know who might decide to sneak in.

While Jelly is quick to slip on her shoes, as Snake ordered. I, on the other hand, am still wondering who this Snake guy really is. Can I trust him? I mean, why would the Hollow Bones want me? Before the carnival, I never knew who the Iron Devils were, let alone the Hollow Bones. They have no reason to come looking for me.

"Was it you?" I ask Snake.

Lifting a brow, he stares at me like I've grown a second head. "Me what?"

"Were you in my office?"

Spreading his legs wide, he crosses his arms over his chest. "Yes, to check for an intruder."

"No." I back up. "Earlier."

Jelly is now staring at me, eyes wide.

Snake looks at the front door, my office door, then at me. "And when would I have gotten in undetected? You saw me sitting across the street."

Yes, I did, but that doesn't mean that he didn't sneak in here. He has a key for crying out loud. Irrational fear crawls under the surface of my skin. I notice that while Snake's attention is on me, Jelly has quietly escaped up the stairs to my bedroom. My phone buzzes with a text. Lifting the device so I don't have to take my gaze off the man in front of me, I open the message.

JELLY:

I'm calling 911 right now.

Thank God. "The cops are on their way. If you're smart, you'll leave."

"Are you serious?" He takes two large steps toward me. "You called the cops on me?" I nod. "Me? I was sent here to protect your ass."

This whole time, I have been slowly backing away. With the next step, I bump into the back door. No doubt, Jelly has already found a way to sneak out of the second-story bedroom window and is waiting for me. Reaching behind me, I open the back door.

That's when I hear it.

Breathing. Low and ragged, and right next to my ear. The hairs on my arm raise, and my eyes widen. That isn't Jelly breathing in my ear. No, that's the breath of an angry man. Now the question is, is this man working with Snake to take us out? Or is this the enemy, and I totally screwed myself by not listening to Snake?

I still have the skillet in my hand, but fear has me frozen. Unable to move. When the cold metal presses into my side, the cast-iron slips from my grip and clatters down the cement steps. "Snake?" My voice wobbles.

He marches forward. A gun aimed right at...me? Is he going to shoot me?

Then, before I can process what's happening, gunshots ring in the air, and a cool rag is pressed to my face. A sweet fragrance assaults my nose before my eyelids become heavy. My arms and legs are starting to feel like lead, and my mind is swimming.

Where am I?

Oh yeah, I'm home with Jelly.

Wait...Jelly. Where is she?

What's happening?

Then...nothing.

My eyes close and refuse to open.

CHAPTER FOURTEEN

Fang

Next to me, Ramon grunts, rubbing his injured leg. The pain is evident on his face. I'd love to send him back to the van, but we can't spare anyone to accompany him. Not to mention, it's a tad too late to turn back now. He wanted in this fight, and now that he's standing just feet away from the enemy's camp, he's locked into this fight.

"You good?" I ask.

"Never better." Pulling the pill bottle from his pocket, he eyes the narcotic.

Knowing his mind is at war with whether to take another or grin and bear it, I ask, "How many you had so far?"

"Four." Well, that's not as bad as I was expecting. I've had four as well to dull the pain in my shoulder. "I'm debating if I need another, or if I should just pop some Ibuprofen and hope for the best."

Since we are about to head into a fight for our lives, I'm going to go with narcotics. With a rookie, I would no doubt make him stay his ass in the van. But Ramon has been the Iron Devils' enforcer since Sinner became the president. I've seen him in combat and shoot while under the influence of pain medicine before. He knows what he can and cannot handle.

"I vote for the one that will kill the pain, but you know what's best for you."

"Yeah." Twisting the cap, he shakes out a pill, dry swallowing.

Zero checks his clips, then cuts his gaze toward us. "You two gonna kiss or you gonna strap up?"

I flip him the middle finger, and Ramon says, "Kiss my ass."

Although I've done this several times, I check all my weapons. Making sure I'm primed and ready. As I go through the motions, my heartrate slows. My mind sharpens and my muscles loosen. That old familiar calm takes over. All other worries slide to the back burner as the warrior within me unleashes.

My mind and body are laser-focused on the task at hand.

Wolf is perching by the window, binoculars in hand, spying on the enemy across the way. Suddenly, he jumps off the rickety old box and waves his hands in the air. Everyone pauses what they're doing to gather in a circle for instructions.

Wolf pulls his Glock from the holster. "It's showtime.

Most have dozed off. As far as I can tell, only two of them are awake. One is playing on his cell, and the other is pacing the front room."

"Copy that." Slipping my Glock from its holster, the cool metal is like a balm to my soul. It steadies me. The familiar weight grounding me. This is the life I was born into. It's the life I was born for.

The grin that spreads on Rage's face is full of vengeance. Full of promise. We are not marching in there blind and hopeless. We're going in with eyes wide open and ready to get justice for our fallen brothers. Rage slips his Karambit knife from the belt holster. The blade of this knife is in the shape of a claw. With a gun in one hand and the combat knife in the other, he says, "I hope they scream."

"Me too." I want the satisfaction of hearing their suffering. To know that they are getting what they deserve. Looking around at our team, each man is poised and silent, ready to attack. These men are not ones to hesitate or question. No, they are tough as steel and deadly as hell. The Iron Devils are not to be messed with.

"What's the game plan?" Sinner questions me.

He's letting me run this show? I thought for sure that once he got back, he would be running things. Maybe this is his way of letting me get the revenge I so desperately seek. "Rage and Zeke flank left. Dash and Hitch flank right. Sinner, Ramon, Haze, you three secure the back and wait for the signal. Zero and Wolf, you're with me. We'll go straight through the front and open fire."

Since this is not our first rodeo, the team knows that once gunfire sounds, that's everyone's cue to charge.

Lifting a hand, I hold up three fingers. Then two. Finally, one. With my fist in the air, everyone stands frozen, waiting for me to open my hand and lower my arm halfway. Our signal to move.

Once the signal is given, the Iron Devils move silently through the night. Wolf, Zero, and I stand in the shadows until the others are in place. Using the binoculars, I spy on the Hollow Bones.

Inside, the only movement comes from the young man leaning against the wall, sipping a bottle of beer. Everyone else appears to be asleep on the floor. One guy is sitting on a rickety old barstool, head leaning against the wall, and a cell phone resting on his thigh.

When the young idiot pushes off the wall and steps into the other room, I motion for my guys to move. As one, we race across the road. Our boots silently thumping against the dirt. Preferably, we want to barge in while the one on guard is out of sight. So far, so good.

Once we reach the door, I peer in the window. When I see that the coast is still clear, I nod, and Wolf carefully pushes the door open, hoping it doesn't creak with the movement. By some miracle, it doesn't. This must be a regular meeting place for the Hollow Bones. It seems the hinges are well-oiled.

We tiptoe into the large saloon, our footstep so light that it makes no sound. Snores echo in the air around us as these men rest on the cold, dusty floor. In the other room, I hear the click, click, click of someone typing a text on their cell phone. Praying that these are all the members in this building, and not any hiding in another room, I motion for Wolf to inch his way to the doorway. As one, we will open fire. Wolf will shoot the guy texting in the other room, while Zero and I start shooting the ones lying on the floor at our feet.

Lifting my weapon, I lock eyes with Wolf, then with Zero. Both are awaiting my signal. Turning my eyes back to the bodies on the ground, I nod, giving them the signal to open fire. At the sound of gunfire, Sinner and the rest of the Iron Devils burst in guns blazing.

Flashes of light blast throughout the room with every gunshot. The noise is deafening to the naked ear. A few men slip their weapons out from their holsters. A redheaded kid, probably no older than twenty, aims from his position on the floor. His gaze is laser-focused on Sinner.

I cannot let my uncle take a bullet. He's taken many for this club, but I'll be damned if he takes one under my charge. Kicking the redhead's arm, the shot hits the ceiling. Taking advantage of his distraction, I aim and shoot. The bullet hits square between the eyes.

Sinner cuts his gaze toward me, a grateful look on his face. He nods but says nothing, not that I would be able to hear a damn thing with all the noise. Out of the corner of my eye, I see an older man inching his way around the bar. He's crouched low to keep out of sight.

As far as I can tell, he doesn't know that I've spotted him. Just as he lifts his arm, I fire. His eyes widen in shock. Dropping his weapon, he touches the base of his throat. When he pulls his hand away, it's covered in crimson. Gripping the countertop, he drops to one knee, opening his mouth to speak. Instead of words, all that comes out is a gurgle.

Slowly, I make my way to the dying man's side, kicking his

leg out from under him. I watch with glee as he falls to his face, gasping for air that will never enter his lungs, thanks to the bullet hole in his neck. With the toe of my boot, I shove him onto his back so I can look into his eyes when I give the final blow.

I recognize this man. He was there the day my brother was shot. Gave me a smirk as he mounted his bike and drove off. "Remember me?" Though words aren't spoken, his eyes tell me all I need to know. He remembers. "An eye for an eye." Standing over him, I aim and shoot. "That's for you, Vile."

Today's elimination is not enough to put my brother or my father at rest. But it's a start. The last gunfire rings in the air. I glance around and see everyone kicking weapons to the side and checking bodies. Sticking my fingers in my ears, I shake them around to try and clear the cottony feeling in my eardrums.

Wolf and Ramon come back into the room, smiles on their faces. Ramon's eyes have dark circles under them. A testament to his hard work despite his painful injury. I wouldn't blame him if he slept for the next couple of weeks. Lord knows I would. "The victory is ours," Wolf shouts.

Ramon nods. "We just did a sweep of the area, all's clear."

Thank God. I'm ready to get home and crawl into my bed. Sleep sounds good right about now. Not to mention, I can't wait to pick up where Winter and I left off. I am so glad this night is over. This war is not over, but at least we gained some ground tonight.

Our plan of action is to head back to the motel, get a few hours' sleep, then head home.

Haze and Zero start gathering the Hollow Bones'

weapons. Sinner pulls out his cell phone to call Dawg. Our prospect will drive the van out here to load the weapons and anything useful left behind. We'll go through everything once we get back to the compound to determine what we'll keep and what will be sold.

As we make the trek back to our bikes, I slip my cell phone out from my back pocket. Pulling up Winter's number, I hover over her name. It's late. She's most likely asleep. Deciding not to wake her, I open the text icon instead.

> Hey, baby. I know it's late, but I wanted to let you know I'm on my way home.

Considering it's about time for the sun to start peeking above the horizon, I don't expect her to answer. So, when my phone buzzes, I'm a little surprised. It's not a text from Winter. It's a call from Snake.

Swiping my thumb across the screen, I answer the call. "Dude, sup?" I'm almost to my bike when he speaks, halting my steps with his words.

"I'm so sorry." I don't like the tone of his voice. He sounds panicked. Not the sound I want to hear from the man I entrusted Winter's care to.

Gripping my cell phone tight, I take a deep breath in an attempt to calm my nerves. "What happened?"

"Winter is gone." Snake sucks in air, like he's in pain.

In the background, I hear a woman. I think it might be Winter's friend, Jelly. "What the hell are you doing?" There's rustling and then her voice comes through the line. "Fang?"

All patience is lost. It went right out the window when

Snake said that Winter was gone. "What the hell happened? Where's Winter?"

"Hey," Jelly's tone grows stern. "Don't yell at me, I'm not the one who pissed in your Cheerios."

Women don't speak to me like that. Ever. The power that comes from being an Iron Devil demands respect. So, I'm taken aback by her tone. "Forgive me, I'm worried about Winter." I pause long enough to rein in my anger. "Where is she?"

CHAPTER FIFTEEN

My head. There's a pounding in my skull like I've never experienced before. *Am I coming down with something?* As I try to swallow, my tongue is stuck to the roof of my mouth. It's almost like I drank too much tequila, and my mouth is dry from all the alcohol. Except, I don't remember drinking. At all.

What happened last night?

Finally opening my eyes, I notice two things. One, I'm not at home in my bed. I'm in a dirty room, tied to a chair. Two, I'm surrounded by several men. None of them is the slightest bit familiar. Then I look at the one sitting in front of me and see the patch on his leather vest. Or cut, as Fang had called them.

Sweat, stale beer, and cigarette smoke taint the air. The stench is horrendous, nearly making me gag. My eyes scan the room, counting heads and searching for an escape. There appear to be six men, all of whom are older and each wearing a sinister smile.

Taking a better look at the man in front of me, or rather the cut he's wearing, I notice the three-piece patch. In the center are crossbones. Their logo, I presume. On the top are the words *Hollow Bones.* Underneath is *Dallas.*

With the flick of a switch, it all comes back to me. I was at my house with Jelly. Snake was outside keeping watch. Until I started hearing noises, then he came rushing in. Something about the situation didn't sit right with me. It all seemed like maybe he was the enemy in disguise. Then, when I was trying to escape, Snake aimed a gun at me and fired.

Remembering the gunshot, I quickly glance down and inspect myself the best I can. Hard to do when your hands are tied behind your back and you're secured to a metal chair. No blood that I can see. That's good.

"Look who's awake." A man with salt and pepper hair and a beer belly snarls. The disgust he has for me baffles me. What did I do to get on his shit list? Well, other than take an interest in Fang. I can see where he would hate me for that. Though he wouldn't know about Fang and me. Unless Snake truly is a traitor. That would be the only way these men would know that.

Which brings me back to my worst fear. Snake is nothing more than a spy and an enemy of Fang.

Oh no, I hope Jelly got away.

I will never forgive myself if Jelly is hurt. She's the sister I never had. The one friend I can never live without.

"Pretty little thing." The man closest to me says. His hair is nappy, and he looks as though he hasn't bathed in days. Gross. Just looking at him, and I need a shower. He is staring at me like I'm a shiny new toy he can't wait to get his hands on. "I can see why the Devils took an interest in her."

Ugh. Gag me with a spoon. This man is repulsive. He had better keep his hands to himself, or I swear to all that is holy, I will gut him with my bare hands. Violence isn't my thing, but I will have no problem putting an end to any of these men who dare lay a finger on me. At the very least, I'll die trying.

The one sitting directly in front of me hasn't said a word. He's leaning back with his ankle crossed over his knee, observing. I can't help but notice how the others glance his way, as if they are awaiting his orders. He must be their leader.

Tugging on the ropes binding me to the chair, I try my hardest to break free. Not that I would have a fighting chance of escaping all these men. They look lethal. I have no doubt they'd tear me limb-from-limb just to hear me scream.

No matter how hard I try, these ropes are not coming loose. Though I didn't really expect them to. I'm sure the Hollow Bones have plenty of experience in tying people up. So, instead of injuring myself further, I cease my tugging and sit up straight, staring at the fearless leader before me.

The dirty one next to me steps closer, the floorboards creaking with the movement. "She's got spirit, can't wait to see it burn out."

Ignoring him, I keep my gaze on the one that matters. "Where is Snake?"

Stubbing out his cigarette, he leans forward with a grin. "Snake? Since when are you familiar with the Iron Devils?"

If he's fishing for information, he'll be sorely disappointed. I will not give him anything. Not even if my life depends on it. "Answer my question."

"You think you wield enough power to talk to our Prez like that?" The guy next to me grabs me by the hair and jerks my head to the side. "You're a nobody who is living on borrowed time." Shoving my head forward, he says, "Prez asks the questions, and you answer."

Giving the greasy creep the death glare, I square my shoulders and give their Prez my attention. He's smirking. If I weren't tied up, I would slap that smirk right off his face. "I said, where is Snake?"

"That asshole got what he deserved." Their Prez stands. Four large steps and he's standing right in front of me. I didn't notice this before because he was sitting, but this guy is tall. Like, I'm talking six feet, four inches or more. I have to strain my neck just to meet his gaze.

Then his words finally register. *That asshole got what he deserved.* Does that mean that I was wrong about Snake being a spy for the Hollow Bones? If that's the case, then why did he point a gun at me? Unless I was mistaken, and the gun was actually aimed at the kidnapper behind me.

Oh no. Did they kill Snake? What about Jelly?

"What do you mean?"

Prez—I hate calling him that, but I don't know his name

—grips my chin vice-like. "What I mean, princess, is that he took a bullet trying to protect what Fang holds dear."

That shot I heard, it wasn't Snake shooting at me. It was the Hollow Bones shooting at him. How did I get this all wrong? I should have trusted the man that Fang put in charge. The man he trusted to keep me safe.

Why didn't I listen to Fang's instructions?

Why didn't I listen to Snake when he urged me to trust him?

My throat constricts with the revelation of my situation. Of Fang's situation once he and the rest of the Iron Devils get back and discover what's happened. Snake is dead because of me. Because of me, the Iron Devils lost a member. Fang lost a brother.

Then a new revelation dawns on me. Fang will hate me for what happened to Snake. I'll be lucky if he doesn't come to kill me himself. Their president must see the fear in my eyes because he cackles, then bends down eye level with me. "Ah, I see you have finally realized the shit you've gotten yourself into." As he speaks, the smell of whiskey and cigarettes infiltrates my nostrils.

He presses his filthy thumb to the corner of my mouth, tracing my lips. "You're such a pretty thing. Too pretty for the likes of Fang." The others watch with glee and laughter. "Do you know what happens to pretty girls like you?"

If only I could turn back time.

"Pretty girls get broken." His eyes light up when a tear falls. Leaning forward, he licks it from my face. "And the tears of pretty girls taste like gold."

Bile burns my esophagus from the touch and smell of him. The Hollow Bones are vile. No wonder Fang and his club hate these men. Aside from the fact that these men killed two very important people to him.

I just want to go home.

Mustering up the courage, I take a deep breath. While he is busy savoring the taste of my tears, I open my mouth and bite the thumb still pressed to my lips. He doesn't yelp, much to my dismay. Instead, he rears his hand back and then slaps me across the face. Hard.

Heat from the impact brings on a new set of tears. I've never been hit so hard in my life. When I open my eyes, the room starts spinning. Cooper floods my mouth. Blood.

Laughter echoes around me. They get a kick out of abusing helpless women. What sick bastards. I hope Fang finds them and burns them alive. Whether he includes me in his rage, I don't care. Not as long as these assholes get what they deserve.

Strong hands grip my shoulders, shaking me relentlessly. "Never been hit before?" He backhands me on the other cheek. "Good. Breaking you in will be fun." A hand closes around my throat, effectively cutting off my air.

Twisting my body and tugging on the rope does no good. I'm firmly held in place. Seconds feel like hours as my lungs struggle to breathe in oxygen. The sound of zippers being pulled and heavy breathing reverberates in my ears.

Are they getting off on watching me get tortured? Jerking off to me being abused. Disgusting.

The harder I try to gain breath, the harder he squeezes.

Soon, the edges of my vision turn dark, and all I can think is, they better keep their hands off me.

Each blink lasts longer and longer.

Fang.

Then blackness.

CHAPTER SIXTEEN

Fang

Wind whips through my hair. The engine is roaring like an angry tiger chasing its prey. After I told my brothers about Snake and Winter, they swore to eliminate the rest of the Hollow Bones. Whether they would have agreed to it or not, I damn sure would have taken them out on my own just for daring to touch what's mine.

White knuckling the handlebars, I zoom through the streets. Every mile is time wasted getting Winter back. Each second in their clutches means another second they can torture her. No telling what she's already endured. I should have never let her leave that clubhouse. She would have been safer behind our walls.

Headlights shine in my mirrors. Our steel horses and

Dawg's van are storming the streets. The Iron Devils are coming in like a tsunami. The Hollow Bones have woken the demon, and we're coming to collect. No stone will be left unturned. Every one of their members will meet their maker.

Winter had better be unharmed, or they will burn under my wrath. The rage running through my veins is venomous, deadly. I'm out for blood.

Thoughts of Winter, scared and alone, force me to up the speed. She doesn't deserve the hand she's been dealt. All because of me. Because I was selfish enough to take her home with me. If I had left well enough alone, she would be happily living her life. Writing some romance novel with cheesy ass men that fall in love too easily.

Being in Hollow Bones territory has my skin itchy. For all we know, they could have men in the shadows, ready to take us out. "Hold on, Winter, I'm coming."

In this moment, every dark thought comes to mind. The torture Winter could be experiencing. How she must hate me for getting her mixed up in my shit. Winter's death at the hands of the Hollow Bones. Yet another person taken from me by those snaky little bastards.

My throat threatens to close up just thinking about her demise. The hairs on my arms rise. These are thoughts I need to push down. They will only distract me from forming a plan. Let's face it, after that phone call, we made a mad dash from the buffer zone to rescue Winter. Planning was the furthest thing from our minds.

Our two-lane road narrows to a single lane. Everyone falls into formation behind Sinner and me. Normally, Wolf would have my position, but I took the lead without asking or waiting for our leaders. Sinner was quick to catch up to me and thankfully did not send me to my rightful spot. Wolf took up behind me, allowing me to take charge of our mission to rescue my girl.

Up ahead is a tunnel. We slow our speed as we wind through the darkened passage. Our engines are like freight trains in the small space. Before long, the tunnel ends, and the road opens back up to two lanes.

Sinner speeds ahead of me. After I got the news about Winter, my uncle sent out an SOS text seeking information on the whereabouts of the Hollow Bones clubhouse. When we stopped to top off our gas tanks, we got the location. It came in pieces from four different sources. One of the sources came from our Houston chapter. Now, here we are on the outskirts of Dallas.

According to one source, we're looking for an old run-down warehouse in a junkyard. Seems about right for those guys. None of them takes pride in anything other than sex and cheap booze.

Taking a left, we enter the side of town where houses are missing paint, and roofs have tarps covering large portions to keep rain out. Some residences have broken-down cars littering the front lawns. Others have grass so tall, there's no telling what critters are lurking around.

When the paved road transitions to dirt, we throttle down to a crawl. This is an area we haven't been in before. No idea what's out here, or if we're even in the right place. Houses are far and few between now. The further we ride, the fewer the houses.

The road curves, and it appears that this area is

completely deserted. Dead crops are rotting away on either side of the road. This is the kind of place the Hollow Bones would enjoy. Quiet enough to torture and kill without drawing attention.

In the distance, I can make out what appears to be a junkyard. The property is surrounded by chain-link fencing. By the looks of it, I would say this is the place. Lifting my hand, I signal the others to stop. Flashing my lights, I gain Sinner's attention.

As one, we pull over on the side of the road. Sinner nods toward the makeshift clubhouse. "I reckon this is the place." All eyes turn to our president as we await his instructions. My legs bounce with the need to get to Winter. "Fang, you got a plan?"

Ramon is leaning against the van, staring at me. A Glock in each hand, waiting for his orders. I take a deep breath. This plan has to go off without a hitch. One hiccup could cost Winter her life.

If she isn't dead already.

I shake off that thought. There is no room for that kind of thinking.

"Wolf and Hitch, y'all go in from the west." The two of them nod, attaching silencers to their weapons. "Sinner, Rage, and Zeke, y'all get the east."

"Copy," Sinner says.

"Dash, Haze, and Zero, march through the front doors." Normally, we don't get prospects involved in these missions. Not on the front lines anyway. But today is a special occasion. "Dawg, you and Ramon are with me."

Dawg's eyes light up. "Yeah? I'm armoring up?"

"You're armoring up." Meeting Ramon's gaze, I say, "We're sneaking in through the back. Kill anyone in the way, but otherwise, our mission is to locate Winter. Once she's found, you're free to unload bullets on every member of the Hollow Bones."

Everyone splits into their groups and begins the trek to the warehouse. All is quiet. Almost eerily quiet. Like they know we're coming. As we get near the large building, I survey the area. Looking for anyone lurking in the shadows of abandoned vehicles or keeping guard on the rooftop.

So far, the coast is clear.

Reaching the back of the building, I notice one of the loading dock doors is wide open. This is not something that would strike me as odd if people were milling about. As I scan the place, all I see is one large open area, apart from a door to the left. The sleeping quarters, I presume.

There is no trace of our enemy anywhere.

Sinner comes out of the only room in this joint. "All clear. Beds are empty."

Beds are empty. Damn. Where are they? I thought this was supposed to be their compound. No club member in their right mind would leave their home vulnerable. Not unless they knew we were on our way and went into hiding.

Ramon, with his expert training, immediately starts searching the place. Looking in places that no human would be hiding in. Which makes me wonder what the hell he's looking for. An icy chill runs through my bones.

A clubhouse void of members.

Ramon is on the hunt for—

Then "Run!" Ramon motions for us to move. At first, I'm

confused, until it dawns on me. The places he was searching, he wasn't looking for a human. It was for a device. A bomb.

Shit.

I sprint as fast as my feet will carry me and don't look back. All around me, footsteps pound the earth. Everyone is running for their lives. Ramon, with his injured leg, is keeping pace with me. We are nearing the road when the explosion bursts my eardrums, and hot waves shove me to the ground.

The ringing in my ears leaves me temporarily deaf. Beside me, Ramon pushes himself off the ground. Fear swims in my gut. This is worse than the time I lost my father. Worse than losing my twin. The unknown, where Winter is concerned, is weighing me down like iron shackles pulling me to the bottom of the ocean.

Pushing myself to my feet, I offer Sinner a hand. He stands and immediately starts looking around. Doing his duty and counting heads to make sure everyone is accounted for. People talk around me, but it's nothing more than marbled voices to my ears. Plunging my fingers in my ear canals, I shake them in hopes of clearing the fog.

Not sure if it helps. Voices still aren't clear.

One thing does ring clear, the way Sinner takes off running toward the burning building. That is the action of a man on a mission to save one of his own. I can feel the color drain from my face as I glance around at my brothers.

Rage, Zeke, Dash, Hitch, Wolf, Ramon, Haze, Zero.

Oh, shit. Dawg is missing. Wolf realizes this at the same time and runs alongside me. By the time we reach the building, Sinner is dragging a severely burned Dawg away from the flames licking skyward.

I skid to a stop when I see his face. An ear is missing, and the skin on his face is like wet pudding slipping away from muscle and bone. Death is no stranger to me. I've been around it my whole life, but this. This is grotesque. The man we were planning to patch in next month is not recognizable. Just a shell of a man.

Dawg is gone.

He's gone, and it's my fault. I was in charge of this mission, and I let a prospect go into battle knowing that lives could be lost. How am I going to look his mother in the eye and tell her that her only boy is gone? Dead. Never coming back.

CHAPTER SEVENTEEN

Fang

A day later, we're riding through the gates of our clubhouse. Entering the gates without Winter is a defeat like none other. To add to my sorrow, Dawg's lifeless body is riding through these gates for the last time. Ramon pulls the van into the garage and then hobbles out. Head down in mourning for our fallen brother.

The weight of his death is going to sit heavily on my soul, just as Vile's does. I'm not sure I'll recover from this one, considering I'm the one responsible for Dawg's death. After I rescue Winter, it will be in her best interest if I cut ties with her. Having no affiliation with me will keep her out of harm's way. I hope.

Sinner opens the back door of the van. Dawg is wrapped

in a tarp, the best we could do with what we had at the time. Buzzcut jogs out with a blanket in hand. No words are spoken. There's none to speak. I take the blanket. Wolf is already removing the tarp when I approach.

Though I've seen his charred body, looking at him now is just as difficult as the first time. Acid rises up my esophagus and burns the back of my throat. Tears spring to my eyes. Yeah, I know men aren't supposed to cry, but this is one exception I'm willing to make. Dawg is deserving of every tear I shed.

"I'm so sorry, Dawg. You deserved so much better." Unfolding the blanket, I spread it over Dawg's body. Sinner leaps into the van to grab his head while I lift him by the legs. Together we carry our fallen brother from the vehicle and to the makeshift stretcher sitting in the corner.

"Did you tell his mother?" Sinner asks Buzzcut.

Buzzcut responds with, "Sure did. Poor thing fell apart right in my arms."

I tune out the rest of the conversation because I cannot deal with this right now. My heart is heavy, and my soul is broken. Needing to get away, I nod to Wolf. "Take over for me, yeah?"

"I'll stay by his side until the funeral home arrives." Wolf takes my place, standing guard over Dawg's body.

Without another word, I trek back to the clubhouse. Visions of the explosion and Dawg's face haunt me. Nothing could have prepared me for this. Yes, we've had war before and lost brothers, but never has the mission been led by yours truly.

It's all a blur as I make my way up to my room. The first

thing I do is grab my journal and hug it to my chest. "I screwed up." I know Vile can't hear me, but a small part of me hopes that he hears me from heaven. "Dude, a prospect died under my command."

I can imagine Vile sitting next to me, gripping my shoulder, saying, "Brother, you can't let this eat you alive. Death is part of our lives. It's inevitable. What happened is not your fault." I want to believe those words, even though they are part of my imagination and not from my twin, I just can't bring myself to accept them.

Time passes as slowly as molasses. The smell of burned flesh still invades my sinuses. Haunting me with my failures. Sitting alone in this room is slowly driving me insane. I have to get out of here. Do something.

As I descend the stairs, I hear voices. Sinner is talking with Wolf about Dawg's funeral. The Iron Devils are covering the cost. Which is what we do. We take care of our own. That will also include providing financial support for his mother.

Avoiding all eye contact, I mosey over to the bar and reach under the counter, grabbing the first bottle my fingers brush against. It happens to be a brand-new bottle of Patron. Forgoing a glass, I uncap the bottle and tip it to my lips.

The burn is a nice welcome. A mini distraction from the hell my life has become. While Sinner and Wolf discuss Dawg's funeral, the others sit around with half-empty beer bottles in their hands. They look about as defeated as I feel.

Buzzcut is standing in the doorway, gazing out like he's waiting for trouble to show up any moment. I pray the Hollow Bones have the guts to show their faces here today. I will gladly rip every single one of them to shreds and then set fire to their remains.

Just thinking about the Hollow Bones brings ill visions to the forefront of my mind. Visions of Winter in some dark, cold cellar, tied up and abused. Some bastard's hand is squeezing her throat, choking the life out of her.

The thought has my chest tightening.

I did this to her.

Pressing the bottle to my lips, I tilt back and guzzle until that tightness starts to ebb away. Then I slam the bottle down on the countertop. Every eye turns my way. They won't say it, but I'm sure they're all thinking it. That Dawg is dead because of me. Winter is held hostage because of me. Hell, even Snake is injured because of me.

Ring. Ring.

Sinner pulls his cell phone from the inner pocket of his cut. Eyes shift my way before he hits answer and walks into the other room. Oh, hell no. Prez or not, that man is not taking a call about Winter without me.

Standing, I march into the other room. Sinner is growling, face red, and hand fisted. Not bothering with politeness, I snatch the phone from his hand and press it to my ear. "Who is this?"

"Well, well, well, if it isn't the golden boy himself." There is no mistaking that voice. Ghost.

"What have you done with her?" I am all out of patience. Club rules? Those flew out the window the minute they involved my girl.

"Now, now, now." What is it with this guy and repeating the same word three times?

"I mean it, Ghost. Where is she?" I'm already pacing in circles, itching to get my hands around his neck.

"Well, she's a lot closer than you think." What the hell does that mean?

"Define close."

A tsk travels through the line, further irritating me. "I'll send directions at dusk." Then the line goes dead.

Sinner takes the phone from my unmoving hand. "What did he say?"

My head is spinning with the information, or lack thereof. How are we supposed to have the upper hand if we are reliant on their directions? If the Hollow Bones are the ones giving us a location, that means they will already have men posted long before we arrive.

What did he mean that Winter is closer than I think?

"Come on." I follow Sinner out of the kitchen and to the chapel doors. "Church. Now."

Everyone scrambles up from their seats and treks to the chapel. We're all exhausted. Wolf takes his seat to the right of Sinner. I sit on the left. Chairs scrape the hardwood floors as men sit around the long oval table.

All eyes are on Sinner, except one. Rage. He is giving me the death glare. Out of all of us, he was the closest to Dawg. The two of them grew up together. I guess he blames me for Dawg's death. Don't worry, man, I blame myself too.

Sinner pinches the bridge of his nose. Blows out a breath. "We lost one man, let's not lose another."

I can feel the angry energy coming off Rage. He didn't get that name by chance. No, this man is a walking, talking time bomb. It doesn't take much to set him off. "Yeah, we lost a man." Rage cuts his gaze back to me. "Because you thought it'd be a good idea to put Fang in charge. Let him play hero for his little plaything, whom he just met."

His words hit me square in the stomach.

Sinner slams his palms on the table. "Watch it."

Rage stands, jamming his finger toward me while talking to our president. "You're the one who put him in charge. He doesn't have the skills. All for what, some whore?"

Never in my life have I seen my uncle stand with such force that it slams his chair to the ground. With a shaking fist, he directs his anger at Rage. "Yes, I put Fang in charge. No, he's not developed the skills I have. That Wolf has. That Ramon has. Hell, Ramon has skills that outrank me." Sinner closes his eyes and takes a breath. "This is how we learn. This is how leaders are made. You think a surgeon has never lost a patient in their first year? We learn and grow from our mistakes."

Rages sits back in his seat.

"Besides," Sinner continues. "When none of the rest of us even considered there might be a bomb, Ramon did. That's because he's trained in that field."

"You're right." Rage slumps in his chair. "You're right." Cutting his gaze toward me, he says, "Sorry, man."

I nod but don't speak. Deep down, I feel that his anger toward me is justified.

Ramon shifts in his seat, adjusting his bum leg to get comfortable. "I was there. Fang did nothing wrong. He assigned us positions. We were already on a mission to eliminate the Hollow Bones. Fang's girl took priority, but nothing in his leadership caused what happened."

Sinner starts laying a plan for tonight. Each of us is listening attentively.

When Ghost sends us details, we'll be ready.

Tonight, we rescue Winter.

Tonight, the Hollow Bones will be no more.

CHAPTER EIGHTEEN

Winter

Cold seeps into my bones. My teeth chatter with enough force that I'm surprised they haven't shattered yet. I'm not sure what I've done to deserve this punishment. The universe must have it in for me. At this point, I'd willingly go back to Halloween night and do things differently.

Actually, no, I wouldn't. Not if it meant not knowing Fang.

A door opens, casting a shadow on the concrete floor. There's laughter somewhere above. Men chanting and clapping. Must be some party they're having while I'm stuck in this icebox below.

The bulb above flicks on, and then there's a click from the door shutting. Footsteps descend the creaky stairs. *Thump. Thump. Thump. Thump.* Glancing around the basement, I notice four deep freezers against the far wall. Images of me being shoved into one and locked away to die flood my mind.

Movement brings my attention back to the staircase. The first thing I notice is dirty and worn biker boots. Pretty much what I've come to expect from this group of bikers. When my eyes travel up, I see the nasty smirk on his face.

In one hand is a medicine bag, in the other is a bucket. Fear of what's to come, I stand and run. Only I don't go far. On my ankle is a shackle. The chain that is attached to the wall pulls tight and forces me to the hard floor. My palms and knees burn from the impact.

He chuckles and sets his supplies on a nearby table. Unzipping his bag, he sets out different tools. Torture devices. Drills, knives, pliers, a syringe, several vials of only God knows what. Fear twists my stomach.

The chain rattling echoes in the empty basement as I inch my way backward. There is nowhere for me to run. No chance of escape. My back hits the concrete wall. Stone bites into my flesh through the soft fabric of my shirt.

The man tips a vial, then plunges the needle into the bottle, withdrawing clear liquid. I watch as he flicks the syringe with a finger. All the while, his gaze has not left mine. His movements are well practiced. This is a man who tortures for a living and loves what he does.

"Don't worry, it won't hurt." A wicked smile brightens his face. "Well, not much."

What the hell is he going to do to me?

"Relax." He sets the syringe on the table. "Boss will be down shortly."

Maybe his boss will take a tumble down the stairs and break his neck.

A creak, a splash of light from upstairs, then the thud of footsteps. The Hollow Bones president appears with a cigarette dangling from his lips. His eyes sparkle with wild fascination. Their leader is one who takes pleasure in others' pain. "Buckle up, buttercup, we're about to go on the ride of your life."

Hopefully, Fang will find me soon. I have no idea what these two have planned for me, but I'm sure it's nothing good.

The first man, the executioner, grabs the syringe. His footsteps are silent as he walks toward me. "Hold still."

Like hell I will. I run to the right, only to come crashing to the concrete floor. Damn this shackle. Pushing up into a sitting position, I tug and tug on the metal that is now biting into my flesh.

Each step he takes, I tug harder. Trying to get away from the evil that is approaching. The president leans against the wall, puffing away on his cigarette. While the executioner gets closer and closer. I don't know what is in that needle, but I'm sure it's nothing good.

At the end of the rope, or rather chain, I have no prayer of avoiding the poison that is sure to be in that syringe. The toe of his boot bumps my knee. Squatting, he grips my chin, squeezing until I fear he'll break a bone.

Anticipation of what's to come eats me alive. Sweat dots my forehead. My heart pounds in my chest. He smiles widely. A grim reaper with dull yellow teeth, ready to rip me open and suck out my soul.

A pinch in my neck startles me. Eyes wide, I stare in

disbelief when he pulls the needle from my neck. Prez chuck-les. It's amazing how fast the poison flows through my veins. At first, it's just hot liquid seeping through my body. Then my heartrate slows. Cobwebs cloud my thinking, and my limbs grow heavy.

When he releases my chin, I fall. It's not like a normal fall. No, it feels as though I'm slowly drifting down to the hard floor. It's like watching a movie in slow motion, only I am the movie. Fear ebbs away. In its place is peace. I watch the executioner with fascination and not a care in the world.

"It's nice, isn't it?" I'm not sure which one spoke. The whole room is mixing into one. Every sound, every movement is all combined into a blob of motion and sound.

In fact, I don't even remember why I'm here. Somewhere in the recesses of my mind, I know I should be scared. I know someone is supposed to come for me, but who is it? When? For the life of me, I can't recall who I'm expecting to come.

The world around me spins. I'm floating.

A face hovers over mine. Like a bad acid trip—not that I've ever done acid—his features morph into streams of color and light. "Relax and enjoy the ride." His voice is too loud, yet not loud enough.

Of its own accord, my body follows his instructions and relaxes. I am one with the air. A giggle slips past my lips. This is nice. No worries. No pain. Just pure bliss. I think I want to stay here forever.

A cloud of smoke blows overhead. Each thread is a different color. Blue, purple, red, green, yellow, and orange. I've never seen anything so amazing. As the cloud of smoke moves, it morphs into shapes. Animals. I lift a hand to touch them, but my hand becomes one with them.

Rippling colors explode, creating a galaxy above. Laughter pulses through the Milky Way. Warmth spreads through my limbs. Boots thud in the distance. Thud to the beat of my heart. *Thud, thud. Thud, thud. Thud, thud.*

"Fang?" His name slips from my mouth, though I don't remember speaking.

Who is Fang? Is he someone important? I try to push through the cobwebs clouding my mind, but I can't seem to break through.

The galaxy shifts, the room expands, and the thudding of boots grows closer. Out of the shadows, a tall form appears. Brown eyes connect with mine. He looks familiar. My heart cries out to him. A combination of cool spices, lavender, and musky woods fills my lungs. It smells like home. Like love.

He crouches down, a smile brightening his eyes. "I found you." Lifting a hand, he traces my bottom lip.

"You found me." My voice is too loud inside my head.

Fang leans forward and brushes his nose against mine. I can't tell you how I know it's Fang, I just do. Kind of like a newborn baby recognizes her mom the first time she's placed in her arms.

"Who the hell is she talkin' to?" The intruder's voice is too far, yet too close. I wish they would go away and leave me alone.

When laughter swirls in the air, Fang grows fainter and fainter. Until he vanishes in a puff of smoke. "Wait," I call out. Yet he doesn't reappear.

The only thing that appears is two bikers. Both are

laughing like they're having the time of their lives. "Dude, she's flyin' high." I'm not sure which one speaks.

My world is still spinning. Sounds turn to colors once more. Euphoria washes over me, and I laugh. I'm not sure why I'm laughing. It just tumbles out of me. The more I laugh, the harder they laugh.

I'm not sure how much time has passed, but my lungs hurt, stomach is tight from laughter. Soon, all laughter fades, and I'm left with deafening silence. Confusion overwhelms me. The air is still swimming in color, but the silence hurts my ears.

A hand wraps around my throat, too tight. My eyes struggle to see the face hovering above me. I blink multiple times. The hand squeezes tighter. Swallowing becomes tough. A flash of red. The cherry of a cigarette. Instinctively, I know it's Prez.

Prez? Is that his real name? I can't remember. It's a funny name. My lips curve in a smile. Who names their kid Prez? Opening my mouth, I try to laugh, but the hand on my throat is cutting off all oxygen.

"God, she's wasted." The man holding my throat takes a puff of his cigarette, blowing smoke in my face. "She needs to come down so we can work on breaking her."

A creak, a flood of light and loud music, then the click of the door. It's all so beautiful when it combines with the streaks sparkling in the air. The hand on my throat releases. There's movement, but I am too distracted to focus. Too distracted to care.

"This her?" That voice sounds familiar. A voice I recognize from my childhood.

"Yep, that's Fang's girl." That sounds like the executioner.

"Good." The newcomer moves closer, gazing at me with hatred shining in his eyes. I know I should be scared, but this warm, fuzzy feeling refuses to let fear in. Instead, I giggle. He lifts a brow. "Damn, how much did you give her?"

"Enough that she was hallucinating just before you came down." Mr. Executioner places a rag over my face.

The fabric tickles, which turns my giggles into a fit of laughter. Water sloshes nearby. If I were in my right mind, I'm sure I'd be terrified. Three faces hover over me. A plastic cup is raised, and I watch as water trickles from the cup to the rag covering my nose and mouth.

Water continues to drip onto the rag until it's completely saturated. As my lungs are slowly being deprived of oxygen, they start to burn. The burn forces me to inhale deeply. Big mistake. Water enters my nose and mouth, filling my airway. I cough and cough, but it does no good. Each time I inhale to try and cough out the water, more enters my lungs.

As I lie here, struggling to breathe, I watch the eyes of these men glaze over. They enjoy seeing me helpless. The one with the cigarette takes a final puff, then places the fiery cherry to my collarbone. Burning registers in my mind, but my body doesn't respond to the pain.

The rag leaves my face long enough for me to draw breath. Then it's back. Once again, water drips onto the rag, slowly drowning me. Laughter echoes in the concrete room. Searing pain slices up my forearm. This time, I do scream, inhaling more water with each breath.

"There she is." Prez leans forward, hand closing around my throat. "I was beginning to think we lost you to the high."

Ripping the rag from my face, he licks my lips like an ice cream cone. Cigarettes and whiskey cling to his breath, making me gag.

Dark hair and hazel eyes come into view. Those eyes look so familiar. Where have I seen this man before? Damn these drugs. My brain is nothing but mush. "I look forward to seeing Fang's face when he gets a good look at you. That punk-ass kid has been a thorn in my side since he learned to talk."

Fang. There's that name again. Fighting these cobwebs in my brain is like cutting down stalks of wheat with a scythe. Laborious and time-consuming. It's like fighting a losing battle. I push and push, but the webs just won't break.

The newcomer narrows his eyes at me. Curling his lip in disgust, he spits on my face. "Filthy Iron Devils trash."

A memory tries to surface. Dark hair and brown eyes. The roar of a motorcycle.

Then another memory fights to surface. Dark hair and hazel eyes. Trips to the ice cream shop. Teddy bears and lullabies.

"It's time," Prez says.

The man with the hate-filled hazel eyes nods, presses buttons on his cell phone, then walks out of the room.

CHAPTER NINETEEN

Fang

Waiting for Ghost to text us a location is like waiting for water to evaporate. I'm surprised I haven't worn a hole in the floor from all the pacing. Not knowing Winter's condition is slowly driving me mad.

"Brother," Ramon places a hand on my shoulder, halting my steps. "Sit down and save that energy. You're gonna need it."

He's right, I just can't bring myself to be still. Hours have felt like eternity. The sun set a long time ago. It's as dark as it's going to get. When is this fool going to call or text with meetup details?

My flesh is crawling with the need to get to Winter. A fire is burning in my gut to murder. Murder is never a term we use. Murder reflects evil. Eliminating the enemy isn't as sinister. It's taking out the trash and cleaning up the world.

Tonight, I'm downright murderous.

A beep echoes in the silent room. All heads turn toward Sinner. He picks his cell phone up from the bar top. I inch forward, hands closing into fists at my sides. "Prez?" I ask, needing to know.

Sinner spins on the barstool, a look of disbelief on his face. As I reach his side, he hands me the phone. On the screen is a location. One I know well. One we all know well. The house across the street from our compound.

How did they get so close without us knowing? Buzzcut is great at keeping tabs on the comings and goings around here. He's always on alert. Hell, we have security cameras all over the inside and outside of our gates.

If they're this close, that means that Winter has been within arm's reach this whole time. God, I could have swooped in and saved the day a hundred times over. Handing my uncle his cell, I march toward the front door.

"Fang, where the hell do you think you're going?" Sinner shouts.

"Where the hell do you think?" I call out over my shoulder. If he thinks he's going to stop me from rescuing my girl, he can think again. Nobody is going to stop me from getting her out of that hellhole.

Ramon falls into step with me. At first, I think he's come to stop me, but he just slips his Glock from the holster on his hip. "Y'all comin'?" he asks the rest.

Neither of us glances back to see who is coming with us.

Chairs scrapping across the floor and heavy footfalls echo

behind us. Sinner says a few choice words, then jogs out the door to catch up with us. The rest of the club members run out, armed to the teeth.

Loud music blasts into the night. As we pass through the gates, I see flashing lights through the windows of the house. This is a setup. We all know it. How can it not be? The minute we walk through those doors, we'll be ambushed. I can feel it deep in my bones.

The streets are deserted, which isn't that unusual around here, considering this is our land. Still, we look left and right before crossing. Ramon has a gun in each hand, both raised and aimed at the house in front of us.

The instant my boots touch grass, gunfire rings out from the upstairs windows. Everyone scatters. Some run for the bushes. Others duck and scramble for cover. Ramon lifts his aim and starts firing. "Move," he screams at me.

Not wasting any time, I hightail it to the house. Leaping onto the porch, I press my back to the siding. I wait a moment, then inch toward the window. I don't want to lean over too soon because I have no idea who is on the other side waiting for my head to appear.

It's a good thing I didn't get in a hurry to look. A shot rings out, and glass shatters next to me. Ramon rushes forward, reloading clips. He drops, rolls, and emerges with guns up, firing shots into the window right next to me.

Despite the loud music, the sounds of bodies dropping like deadweight meet my ears, bringing a smile to my face. Sinner jumps onto the porch with a groan. His old joints don't take the impact like they used to. Using his body-weight, he kicks the door in, sidestepping out of the way in case there's a Hollow Bones member waiting in the shadows.

Wolf appears from the left of the house. Sinner and I glance over. He holds up two fingers, indicating that there are two men in the living room, armed and ready.

Ramon drops down and arm crawls toward the door. With a kick of his foot, he slides forward, firing into the house. When there is no return fire, Ramon stands and rushes through the doorway.

I take off after him, Sinner and Wolf close on my heels. Wolf and Sinner split to cover the downstairs. Ramon takes the stairs two at a time, and I follow. The others can be heard entering the front door, boots crunching on glass as they move.

As we reach the top, the smell of stale cigarettes and piss assaults my nose. Don't get me wrong, our clubhouse never smells like fresh linen, but it doesn't smell like rot and decay either. This is nasty. Even the carpets are stiff from years of grime.

Ramon moves slowly and steadily. Glancing down the hall, he lifts a hand, two fingers raised. Signaling two doors. Behind me, footsteps pad the carpeted stairs. Rage. Even though he is pissed at me over Dawg's death, he's here to cover our six.

Moving toward the first door, Ramon grips the knob, nodding for me to be ready. Lifting my gun, I aim at the door, waiting for Ramon to twist the knob. As soon as the wooden door swings open, I brace myself for gunfire. When there is none, I march into the room. Rage trails in behind me, searching under the bed. Ramon searches the closet.

"Clear," Ramon says. Snatching the pillow off the bed, he

takes the lead. The second door is on the opposite side of the hall. Ramon motions for Rage to open the door.

Moving to the other side of the door, Rage twists the knob and throws the door wide open. Ramon tosses the pillow into the room. Three shots, rapid fire in the direction the pillow went. Motioning for Rage and me to stay put, he lifts both guns and steps into the doorway, firing.

As soon as bullets stop flying, I rush into the room fully expecting to find Winter tied to a chair in the corner. Instead, I'm met with an elbow to the face when the closet door swings open and a young kid comes out screaming his battle cry. He doesn't look a day over eighteen. I'm not sure if he's one of them or an innocent.

Using the butt of my gun, I clock him upside the head. He falls to the floor, then glares up at me. Grabbing a handful of hair, I lift him to his feet. At first, the kid looks like he's about to punch me, but the sight of Ramon aiming both guns at him and Rage standing with arms crossed and a gun in hand, has him thinking twice. "Where is Winter?"

He laughs. "I ain't telling you shit, Devil."

That right there is all the proof I need that this punk is a Hollow Bones. "Wrong answer." I punch him in the nose hard enough that bones crack. "Try again."

The kid spits blood and smirks. This won't do. In one swift motion, I holster my gun, grip his wrist with one hand, and his elbow with the other. Pressure on the elbow as I twist the wrist back wipes the smirk right off his face. I keep adding pressure until I hear the pop of bones.

A scream rips from him as his arm breaks. "Okay, okay."

I cease adding pressure, but don't release him. "Where is Winter?"

"Base...basement." Now that we know where my girl is, I release my hold on him. The second his body falls to the ground, Ramon presses the trigger, putting a bullet right between the kid's eyes.

A splatter of blood hits my cheek. Do I care? Not in the slightest. That punk deserved what he got, and I will proudly wear the remnants. The beast inside me thrives off it. As if the kid's death is tied to the blaring music, the thumping ceases, and all is quiet.

The crunch of the sticky carpet can be heard with each step I take. Knowing that Winter is just two floors below me has my feet moving faster than they have ever moved. As the club's enforcer, Ramon is always a step ahead and ready for trouble. He jogs down the stairs, jumping the last four steps with a groan.

Sinner skids to a stop when he sees us descending. "Where is she?"

"Basement," I say.

Rage jumps over the banister midway down. "Ground floor all clear?"

"Yes." Wolf enters the room, reloading a new clip into his weapon.

"We gotta find the basement door." Those doors are generally toward the back of the house, usually around the kitchen.

I'm already moving in that direction when Ramon shouts, "Over here."

When we enter the kitchen, Ramon is standing next to an

open door. Zeke and Haze are walking up the basement stairs. Zeke meets my gaze, "No one's down there."

My heart hammers in my chest. Where else would she be? That kid said she was down here. "Any signs that she was here?" I refuse to believe that kid lied, and we killed him before getting the truth out of him.

Zeke nods. "Other than a shackle attached to the wall, a vial and syringe, and some blood smears, I found this." He hands me a bracelet.

My heart immediately skips a beat. This is Winter's bracelet. I remember her telling me about her mother giving it to her before cancer took her from this world. "It's hers." Clutching the thin gold bracelet to my chest, I step over bodies, needing fresh air. Every nerve in my body is stretched tight.

The night air is calling my name. Exiting through the back door, I nearly crumble to the ground. How could this happen? Winter can't be the third person in my life I lose to this life. No, not the third person. Dawg's life was taken. Winter would be the fourth. I swear, if they have killed her, I will set fire and burn the whole world.

Buzzing in my back pocket has me scrambling to fetch my cell phone. It's a text from an unknown number.

UNKNOWN:

Now that I've got your attention. How about we play a little game?

Game?

Bring her to me, and she better be
unharmed.

I know Ghost. He enjoys watching people suffer. The man I once thought of as an uncle is now my biggest enemy. Not just because of Winter, but my father, Vile, and Dawg as well. As soon as I find out where that bastard is, I am going to strangle him slowly, then light his ass on fire. When I'm done with him, he'll be nothing but ashes.

UNKNOWN:

No promises there.

I can hear voices inside. Sinner is having a meeting with the club members. That's not important right now. What is important is finding Winter and ending the Hollow Bones for good.

Where's Winter?

UNKNOWN:

Closer than you think.

What the hell? Not this again.

Stop toying with me. Where is she?

UNKNOWN:

Now, now. That's not the attitude of a good
player.

I swear to all that is holy, if Ghost doesn't stop with the

bullshit, I'm going to rip out my hair. Knowing he won't stop until I decide to play along, I give in.

> What game are we playing?

UNKNOWN:

> We are playing a little game of rescue the cat.

> Fine. What are the clues?

UNKNOWN:

> Start from home?

Start from home? Is he referring to my childhood home? What home?

> Define home.

UNKNOWN:

> It's staring you in the face.

Sinner is in the middle of some speech, every ear listening intently, when I come crashing through the door. Wolf and Ramon are the first to shift their attention. Ramon's eyes widen when he sees the state I'm in. "What is it?"

I toss him the phone. "She's at the clubhouse."

"Shit." Sinner lifts a hand, motioning for us to follow. "Let's move."

CHAPTER TWENTY

Winter

Boots shift. The sound stirs the acid in my stomach, making me nauseous. My body is still too heavy to move. I'm helpless lying on this cold, wet floor. I cough and cough. Water is still lingering in my lungs, burning.

Prez still stands next to me, lighting another cigarette like this is just another Friday night. Hell, maybe it is. The executioner appears at my other side with a metal tray in hand. I have no idea what is on it, but the gleam in his eye tells me it's nothing good.

Overhead, the bare bulb swings when the executioner bumps it with his shoulder. He laughs when I gag from the motion of light. "I see you're starting to crash." Kneeling beside me, he says, "Better get you back on that high, sweetheart."

No, I don't want any more of whatever drug he pumped into my veins. That is some wicked stuff, and I don't like the ill effects it has on me. The glint of light on metal has me twitching to get away.

Prez steps on my left arm to hold it down while the man with the syringe grabs my other arm, jabbing the needle into the vein in my inner elbow. Warmth shoots up my arm, and it only takes two seconds for the heat to dull all my senses.

Then I'm just floating. No pain. No cares. Just me and bliss.

Metal jingles. The shackle around my ankle moves. A key slides into the lock, and the heavy metal falls away. My leg twitches with the newfound freedom. It's nice. Almost as nice as taking off your bra at the end of the day.

Warm hands slide under me, lifting me off the cold floor. "Just enjoy the high while we take a little trip."

His words drip around me like melted butter. Not sure how that's possible, but here I am watching his words drip like liquid butter on popcorn. I'm not sure who is carrying me. Faces are nothing but a blur at this point.

Opening my mouth to speak is a chore. The signal from my brain to my lips seems to have gotten lost along the way. Not to mention my tongue is thick and heavy, and my throat is drier than the desert.

A strange noise escapes my lips.

Laughter. I'm not sure who is laughing. It could be both men. Or is it three men? I can't remember. "Don't strain yourself, sweetheart. Just enjoy the ride."

Jostling twists my insides. My stomach heaves, but nothing comes up. A door opens. Light floods into the room, and music hurts my ears. Faces gaze at me. Laughter rings out all around. Someone calls for Ghost, and the inner parts of my brain register the name.

"Ghost, this is your rodeo. Take her and do with her as you will."

"Yes, Prez." The man named Ghost smirks at me. It's distorted and evil. Then he looks at the man holding me. "Rat, you're with me."

Rat? I squint, trying to see the face of the man holding me. It takes great effort, but I finally recognize him as the one I call the executioner.

The man holding me, Rat, nods. "You got it, VP."

Movement plays tricks on my vision as we travel through the house. Then cool air hits my skin. My wet clothes turn frigid from the drop in temperature. Ghost laughs from somewhere nearby. Stars twinkle in the darkness above.

One minute there are stars, the next they're gone. I squint, trying to find them because they're pretty to look at. All I see is shades of green, yellow, and red. The color of fall leaves. Oh, those are beautiful. I'm so lost in the colorful leaves that I don't notice the sound of gunfire at first.

The jostling gets intense, and soon the pretty leaves are no more. Stars shine down on me once again. Then the movement stops, and a hand slaps over my mouth. My eyes grow wide. A creak of metal. Soft footfalls on the ground. The click of a door.

Sweat starts to dampen my face and neck. Not because I'm hot, I'm not. My body is still shivering from the cold. Hot liquid rises in my throat, and the bitter taste of bile hits my tongue. I can't spit it out. There is still a hand pressed to my lips, so I swallow.

A shadow appears in my peripheral vision. Ghost's voice is too loud to my own ears. "Time to move."

Bright light nearly blinds me. The thumping of boots on tile meets my ears as we move through the house. I hear chair legs banging on the floor, like someone is thrashing it around in a fit of anger. Cracking an eye open, I look for the source of the noise. In the corner of the room, a big, burly man is tied to a wooden chair. Duct tape is over his mouth and wraps around his head to secure it in place.

On the opposite side of the room is another chair. Rat sets me down on it, and Ghost begins wrapping rope around my torso to keep me from falling off. My legs get tied next, then my hands are bound behind the back of the chair.

Because I have no control over my body, my head lolls to the side. "God, she's pathetic." Ghost grabs a handful of hair and lifts my head. "You ready to bring that boyfriend of yours to his knees?"

Do I have a boyfriend? Wait, flickers of memory try to surface through the fog. Brown eyes. But they're not the brown eyes that make me weak in the knees. No, these eyes leave a bad taste in my mouth. Billy. My ex.

Gross.

More and more memories start to trickle in now that I'm glancing around at this familiar room. Jelly, my best friend. Halloween night. A biker carnival. Haunted houses and black angel wings. Wings on a bare chest that smells of cool spices, lavender, and musky wood.

Fang. Yes, Fang was my fallen angel on Halloween. "Fang." My tongue is thick, and the word is garbled as it falls from my lips.

Ghost chuckles. "Yes, we're about to play a little game with that asshole boyfriend of yours."

CHAPTER TWENTY-ONE

Fang

Rage keeps pace with me as we run out the front door. His anger at me is on the back burner for now. Thank God. He's got his Glock in hand, ready for whatever we're about to walk into. Ghost likes to play sick games. For all I know, Winter could be halfway across the country by now.

The gate to the compound is locked, as it should be. Sinner reaches into his jeans pocket for his keys, fumbling with them once he has them in hand. "Damnit." Finally steadying his hand, he gets the key in the lock. Wolf and Zero push the heavy iron gates open. The metal groans with the movement.

I don't wait for them to get it wide open. As soon as there's enough room for me to squeeze in, I do. Rage is right behind me. The two of us rush to the clubhouse, guns at the ready.

Lifting my leg, I kick the door in. Could I have tried the doorknob? Yeah, but I don't want to waste time. Bursting in seems the better way. At least that's what I'm telling myself. When the door crashes into the wall and I get a look at the scene before me, my heart drops to my toes.

"Holy shit." Rage's voice floods with panic.

On one side of the room, Buzzcut is gagged and tied to a chair. Blood trickling down his face from a cut on his temple. Ghost, a man I haven't seen since I was a kid, holds a knife to Buzzcut's throat.

That's not what has my heart skidding to a stop. On the other side of the room, a nearly unconscious Winter is tied to a chair. Sweat dampens her hair, and her head lolls to the side. Her eyes are unfocused, and she looks almost peaceful.

What the hell did they do to you?

A man I don't recognize is standing behind Winter, a syringe in hand. I lift my weapon, ready to shoot the bastard who dares to harm my girl. "Uh, uh." Ghost smiles. "You shoot him, and they both die."

"Talk," I say, voice stern and full of rage.

"You see," Ghost says. "We have your little girlfriend tied to a mechanism. You shoot Rat, and I press this button right here." He shows me the device in his free hand. "Attached to the back of her chair is a spear. With the touch of my finger, it goes through her heart."

Fear turns my bones ice cold. One wrong move and Ghost will kill not just my brother, but my girl as well. Rat flicks the syringe with a finger to remove the air bubbles.

Damn, what's in that needle, and how much has he already given her?

"What do you want?" This man has already taken so much from me. He has ruined my life.

Ghost smirks. "I want to take everything from you, just like your father took everything from me."

"What the hell are you talking about?" Ghost is delusional. "What did my father ever take from you?"

Ghost's lip curls in a snarl. "Your father stole my wife."

"Your wife?" My father was loyal to my mother until his last breath. "I think you've hit your head one too many times. My father was in love with my mother. He never once strayed."

"Ah, yes, the ever-loving husband." He makes a gagging face. "Your mother was my wife first. We were happy and in love."

What the hell? That can't be right. Shaking my head, I say, "My mother was never married to you."

"Oh, but she was."

"If my father stole your wife, then why did you stick around and play the part of his best friend? Why would you treat me as a nephew?" It doesn't make sense. And why didn't my parents ever tell me? If Ghost was Mom's ex-husband, why would she let him buddy up to my dad, to me? Oh god, tell me I'm not related to this asshole. Mom didn't cheat on Dad, did she?

"Because I loved your mother."

The contents of my stomach start to churn. "Please tell me you're not secretly my father."

"Absolutely not." He spits like just the thought of me as

his son makes him sick. I feel the same way. "Your mother was loyal to a fault."

I glance over at Winter. Rat is still behind her, holding the syringe, waiting for orders to inject her with that poison. "So, what, you want to kill Winter because my mother chose another man over you?"

He chuckles. "I want to bleed you dry the same way Grimm bled me." Glancing over at Winter, he smirks. "But I'll tell you what, I'm willing to let her go if you play a game with me."

"What game?"

Ghost smiles widely. "You pick who dies."

"What?" Rage and I yell.

"Yep." Ghost digs the knife into Buzzcut's neck until crimson pebbles under the blade. "Buzzcut, Rage, or your girlfriend."

He's going to make me choose between two brothers and my girl. I can't do that. Club law demands that I protect my brothers at all costs. Choosing to have one executed can get me stripped of my patch. Not only that, if the club agrees, that could mean my execution.

Dropping my shoulders, I glance back at Winter, feeling utterly defeated. "You know I can't make that decision."

Ghost's smile widens. He knows he has me by the balls. "Then it looks like your girlfriend and your brother are both dead."

"Wait." I drop to one knee. Begging is not in my blood. It's not in any brother's blood. Begging is for the weak. "Don't kill her, she's innocent."

"Innocent?" Both Ghost and Rat laugh. "Anyone who is

associated with the likes of you is not innocent." Wiggling a finger like a metronome, he tsks. "Tick tock, Fang. Time is running out. Choose."

Winter groans. Rat watches her with delight, like he enjoys torturing her with his poisonous needle. He probably does. The Hollow Bones are sick freaks. Her eyes are glassy, but they zero in on my face. "F—Fang?"

"Yes, baby, I'm here."

Rat's hand inches toward Winter. I can't let him jab her with that toxin, but I can't stop him without Ghost retaliating. Ghost rolls his eyes. "How touching." The tone of his voice mocks. "Who will it be, Fang?"

Winter's brows furrow. Like a sloth, she turns her head to look at Ghost. She squints, studying his features. With a gasp, her eyes widen. Recognition shining in the depths of those hazel pools. "Oh my god. It's you."

CHAPTER TWENTY-TWO

Winter

My head is swimming. A jackhammer is wreaking havoc on my skull. Still, his voice calls to me, forcing my eyes open. Lifting my head is challenging. It must weigh a hundred pounds. With great effort, I manage to lift it enough to see him. The man who visits me in my hallucinations. Fang.

No matter how hard I try, I can't get my eyes to focus enough to see if he's really here, or if this is another hallucination. Everything is a big blur, but I know he's here. I can feel his presence. "F—Fang?"

"Yes, baby, I'm here." His voice is like a balm to my soul. I try to reach for him, but my arms won't budge. Rope rubs against my wrists. Seems I'm tied up like cattle.

"How touching." That voice. It seems so familiar, and not

because I've been listening to him all night. I know that voice. "Who will it be, Fang?"

Sweat drips from my hairline as I struggle to turn my head. I know I saw his face earlier, but I can't help but feel like we're old friends. The man is standing across the room. Too far away for me to see his face. My vision is still cloudy from the drugs. Squinting, I lean forward as much as I can, doing my best to focus.

Little by little, his features become clear. For the first time tonight, I recognize the man standing across from me. The one who laughed at my demise. Dark hair, dirty and unkempt. Hazel eyes that I once loved. My heart stills. It can't be. How could a man who once loved me hurt me so cruelly?

I gasp because I can't believe my eyes. "Oh my god. It's you."

The man everyone calls Ghost sneers my way. "Yeah, I've been me all night long."

"But why?" Make it make sense. This cannot be happening.

"Because you're Fang's." His tone is full of disgust and rage.

"So, you would kill your blood because I'm dating your enemy?" Am I really that worthless to him?

"My blood?" All color drains from his face. "Wait, your name is Winter?" His eyes stare into mine like he's searching my soul. Whatever he's holding in his hand falls to the floor. "You're Winnie?"

Tears fill my eyes, and for the first time in my life, I know what betrayal tastes like. What happened to the man I once knew? The one who bought me gifts and took me out for ice cream. "Yes, Uncle Josh, it's Winnie."

"Uncle?" Three voices ask in shock.

Whizz-crack.

The sound catches me off guard. It's quickly followed by a loud gunshot. I watch my uncle crash to the floor, blood oozing from a hole in his neck. Behind me, a thump quickly follows my uncle's fall. Did someone shoot Rat? Man, I sure hope so. I'm ready for this nightmare to end.

Boots thud on the hardwood. Next thing I know, Fang is kneeling in front of me. "You okay?"

"Uh, huh." Suddenly, I'm so tired. My body shakes uncontrollably, and sweat drips from my pores like a leaky faucet. My arms feel like they're going to break when the rope is jerked back. Seconds later, the bothersome rope falls away, and its sweet relief.

Fang is cutting away at the rope binding my legs to the chair. As soon as he gets me loose, he lifts me in his arms. "I've got you."

Closing my eyes, I rest my head against his chest, smelling the scent that has quickly become my favorite smell. The sound of the Iron Devils gathering around meets my ears, but I can't bring myself to open my eyes and thank them. That will have to wait until morning. Right now, I need sleep.

I hear Rage telling Sinner about Ghost being my uncle. There are loads of questions that follow, but my mind is vastly drifting off. Voices get fainter as we move through the house. A door is shoved open, and then I'm being laid on a soft mattress.

When his arms leave my body, I cry out, "No, don't leave."

The last thing I want is to be left alone. What if the Hollow Bones come for me again? There's no way I stand a chance against them in my current state.

"I'm not goin' anywhere, baby." Fang kisses my forehead. "But I do need a shower, I'm covered in blood."

"No." I reach for him, but my hand falls to the mattress like lead.

There's a pause, and I think he's left me anyway. Then I hear the rustle of fabric. The bed dips, and then warm arms wrap around me. "You're so cold." Sitting up, he tugs the blanket over us, then pulls me flush against his bare skin.

He mumbles against my hair, but I'm too tired to understand. Nuzzling into his side, I finally allow the darkness to claim me. With Fang next to me, watching over me, I know I'm safe. The Hollow Bones can't get to me as long as he's here.

Thoughts of Uncle Josh follow me into dreamland. The good guy I knew as Uncle Josh was my hero. Ghost was a monster. Both versions of him plague my dreams.

CHAPTER TWENTY-THREE

Fang

"Oh my god. It's you." Winter's voice is weak, but what does she mean? Has she met Ghost before? What the hell is going on?

Ghost sneers at her. "Yeah, I've been me all night long." The way he dares to speak to her, I could tear him limb-from-limb.

A sadness washes over Winter's features. "But why?" The way she asks, it's almost like she's heartbroken over this fool. Which is something I just can't wrap my head around.

Ghost's top lip curls in disgust. "Because you're Fang's."

That's right, asshole, she's mine.

"So, you would kill your blood because I'm dating your

enemy?" Wait, what did she just say? Is Winter insinuating that she is related to Ghost?

"My blood?" Ghost pauses, his eyes staring at her like he's seeing her for the first time. Then all the color drains from his face. "Wait, your name is Winter?" If at all possible, his face loses more color, and he looks like he may toss his cookies any minute. To my relief, he drops the device that could kill Winter. "You're Winnie?"

How the hell did I get mixed up with my enemy's blood? Shocked doesn't begin to describe how I'm feeling. My mind automatically thinks that Winter has been a spy for Ghost. Was it really a coincidence that we met on Halloween? But as I watch tears fill her eyes and the look of betrayal that shines in those hazel pools, I know she knew nothing of Ghost's extracurriculars.

"Yes, Uncle Josh." Those tears break free, wetting her cheeks in their descent. "It's Winnie."

"Uncle?" Rage, Rat, and I ask in shock. How is Ghost her uncle, and how did she not know who he was in the MC world? Then it dawns on me. He did not recognize her the entire time he held her captive. That means he hasn't seen her in ages, probably since she was a kid. Which would explain how she had no clue who Ghost was.

Before I know what's happening, I hear the sound of a bullet whizzing nearby. When Ghost clutches his neck, blood spurting from a hole there, I know Ramon has made his move. With a quick hand, I put a bullet between Rat's eyes. Rat hits the floor two seconds after Ghost.

Rage and I run forward. He rushes to free Buzzcut, and I

rush to free my girl. My very drugged-out girl. God, what the hell did they give her? "You okay?"

Winter's glassy eyes struggle to connect with mine. "Uh, huh." She looks so wasted. Her body is shaking uncontrollably, and sweat is dropping from her pores. I have to get these ropes off her and get her up to my room to sleep this shit off.

Once her arms are free, her body slumps forward, and I use my forearm to keep her somewhat upright as I kneel to cut the rope binding her legs to the chair. It takes a little longer than I'd like, but I finally get her untangled. Lifting her into my arms, I realize just how hot her body is. She's burning up. "I've got you."

The second the words leave my lips, her body becomes lax. Her head rests against my chest, and her lungs inflate. I'd like to think she's pulling my scent into her lungs. Or it could be the fact that she feels safe at last, and her body is just releasing tension.

Boots stomp up the porch steps. I don't need to turn around to know it's my brothers. Ramon approaches with a major limp in his step. "She okay, brother?"

I nod. "She will be, they have her hopped up on something." Glancing down at Rat, I say, "Search his pockets. If you find a vial, be sure to let the doctor know when he gets here."

"Will do." Ramon joins Sinner and Wolf, discussing what to do with the remains of Ghost and Rat. I don't care what they do with them. Burn them, chop them to pieces, and feed them to the pigs on the farm just outside of city limits. As long as I never have to lay eyes on them again, I'm good.

As I start up the stairs, I hear Rage filling Sinner in on Ghost's relation to Winter. Several questions follow. "She's related to that piece of shit?" "Is she one of them?" "Did he send her Fang's way to spy on us?"

I tune them out. This can all wait until tomorrow, when everyone's had time to rest and think clearly. My priority is getting these drugs out of Winter's system and making sure she's okay. The Hollow Bones have ripped her clothes to shreds, and I can see several cuts and a few cigarette burns on her flesh.

A girl working with the enemy would not have suffered as she has. They tortured her. Tried to break her for their own sick and twisted minds. They did a real number on her. After seeing the damage, I'm glad we got rid of the Hollow Bones for good.

It takes some doing, but I get my hand free enough to twist the doorknob. Using my foot, I shove the door open and trek to the bed so I can lay her down. Up to this point, she's been softly snoring, but the moment her body hits the mattress, those eyes flutter and she cries out. "No, don't leave."

"I'm not goin' anywhere, baby." I bend over to kiss her forehead. "But I do need a shower, I'm covered in blood." It's not an over-exaggeration. I am wearing Hollow Bones blood like a second skin.

"No." She outstretches her hand, reaching for me, but it falls like lead.

I stand still, just watching her, debating whether to take that shower. Then I think back on how alone I felt when Vile died. How I wanted nothing more than to feel Sandra next to me. We had both lost my brother, and for days we lay in bed, soaking in the comfort of the other. There's no way I can leave Winter knowing how desperately she needs me.

Stripping off my clothes, I crawl into bed beside Winter. In contrast to how hot she was just moments ago, she is absolutely frigid now. "You're so cold." Thank God I never made my bed. The blanket is rolled up at the bottom. Sitting up, I grip the thick material and pull it over our bodies. As soon as I pull her body flush with mine, the shivering stops, and she snuggles into my arms. "You've stolen my heart, Winter Green. I am forever yours."

I'm just dozing off when I hear my bedroom door open. After the last few days, I'm quick to untangle myself from Winter and hop out of bed, snagging my Glock off the nightstand. Doc holds up his hands. "Sorry, Fang."

Lowering the gun, I ask, "Why the hell didn't you knock?"

"I did." He glances over at Winter. "I knocked for quite some time. When I didn't get a response, I figured I would let myself in and make sure you were both alive." He moves to her side of the bed and places the back of his hand to her forehead. "No fever, that's good."

Now that I know we're safe, I crawl back into bed with Winter. "Should I wake her?"

Doc nods. "You can try to wake her, but I wouldn't be surprised if she's out for the count. The drugs they injected her with were a mix of opioids and a sedative. She may not rouse, so don't freak out."

Gently shaking her, I do my best to wake her. No matter how hard I try, she doesn't budge at all. I know Doc said she may not stir, but I can't help but freak out. Internally. "Please, help her."

"I will." He opens his medicine bag, rummaging through the contents. When his eyes meet mine, he says, "You may want to step out."

"Like hell I am." This man has lost his mind if he thinks I'm leaving him alone with her. What happens if she wakes up and I'm not there, but a complete stranger is standing over her, examining her?

"Suit yourself, but this may not be an exam you want to witness." I lift a brow because this man knows the shit we do. Each of us has been through hell and back. A few wounds and burns are not going to make me weak in the knees. Then he says the one thing that guts me. "In addition to the obvious, I need to examine her for rape."

That word echoes over and over in my head. If the Hollow Bones weren't all dead, I would run out of this clubhouse and hunt down every last one of them. Thankfully, we got them all. And I will make no apologies for their demise.

"I'm staying."

Doc nods and begins treating her wounds. I lift Winter's hand and thread our fingers together. This day will haunt me for the rest of my life. Especially if Winter wakes up and decides this is not the life for her. That would be my undoing. Living in this world without Winter by my side would be too much. I'm not sure I could stay here if she weren't with me.

Dread fills me at the thought of her not wanting me.

Doc works swiftly, and I take note of all the wounds that had been hidden under parts of clothing. There are so many more cuts than I first thought, and some bruising I hadn't noticed before. Looks like she had been kicked in the stomach several times.

"Good news." Doc places a bandage on the last open wound. "There doesn't appear to be any broken bones, and these lacerations should heal with minimal scarring."

Relief floods me, and I feel thankful that her injuries aren't worse.

"Now, I need to do a vaginal exam." His words knock the wind out of me, reminding me that we aren't done yet. She could still show signs of worse injuries.

God, I know I've never been a praying man, but please let Winter come through this. Please let there be no signs of rape.

I don't know if God exists, but right now I hope he does. I need him to exist. To fix Winter.

Doc takes instruments out of his bag. They look cold and sterile. I can't watch. Turning Winter's head so we're face-to-face, I focus on her. Her scent, her nose, those full lips. If this is the last time I get to hold her, I want to memorize every feature. Also, if she happens to wake up while Doc is examining her, my face is what I want her to see first. So, I can reassure her that everything is okay. That I've got her.

It doesn't take him long. Next thing I know, Doc is packing up. "Fang, she got real lucky."

Peeling my eyes away from Winter, I glance at Doc with hope. "So, you're saying that she wasn't—" I can't even let the word slip from my lips.

Doc nods. "There are no signs of rape."

"Thank God." I nearly collapse in bed with relief.

Winter was not violated. Now I can close my eyes and get some sleep.

CHAPTER TWENTY-FOUR

Winter

It's been two weeks since I saw Fang. After being kidnapped by his rival gang, club, whatever the hell they call it, I couldn't stay there. Yes, Fang, Sinner, and Buzzcut all reassured me that the Hollow Bones could never hurt me again, but what's to say that another rival club won't do the same?

I'm a writer. Violence in the real world is not for me.

"Hello?" Jelly's voice echoes through the quiet house. My best friend has made a point to check on me multiple times a day. Also, she's been spending time with Snake. Speaking of, I had a nice, long conversation with Snake after I had time to recover. I needed to apologize for my accusations and behavior. All of which he was quick to forgive.

"I'm in the office." With all the events that happened in

the last couple of weeks, my imagination has run wild. In two weeks, I have written a one hundred twenty thousand word romance novel. Of course, the main male character is based on Fang.

Speaking of Fang. He calls every day. Every time he calls, I let it go to voicemail. I just don't know if I can let him back into my life knowing that danger will always be lurking around the corner.

Jelly bounces into the room carrying a greasy bag. That greasy bag can only mean one thing. Burgers and fries from Mick's Diner. Not the same diner, as that one was destroyed. But they did buy a new building and reopened to the public. They do make a mean burger, but it also brings back memories of Fang and me.

Every day she brings food from Mick's. I would tell her to stop, to pick up food from literally anywhere else, but when Jelly buys you food, you eat that food. In the words of my best friend, *I bought that for you, and you're gonna eat it and enjoy it.*

So, here I am, standing to follow her to the kitchen. Neither of us bothers with plates. We use the burger wrapper as a plate of sorts. Mick's Diner has the best food on the planet. Does it make me sad when I see the logo? Hell yes. Do I regret eating from there? No, not when that first bite hits the taste buds.

So. Freaking. Good.

Ding.

I look up to see Jelly dropping her burger like it just bit her. Only to dig her cell phone out of her purse like it's her next booty call on the line. Popping two fries in my mouth, I watch as her entire face lights up, reading the text that came through.

"Okay," I say around a mouthful of fries. "Who is texting you?"

"Oh, it's no one." But as she replies, I can see that it most certainly is someone. Then she bites her lower lip.

"Okay, Jelly-Bean, spill." She doesn't tear her eyes off the screen, and when her cell phone dings again, pink tints her cheeks. "Are you sexting at my dinner table?"

"Sorry, it's just Snake." She sends off another reply, then slips the phone back in her purse.

"You're sexting Snake while sitting at the dinner table with me?" Gross.

"Yes." She picks up her burger, taking a massive bite. I'm not sure if she took such a big bite to avoid answering questions or because she's hungry.

"And how long has that been going on?" I know they've been hanging out, but I didn't realize it was like that. What I don't want is for her to feel like she has to hide parts of her life because of me.

"Since the day he was shot."

The day he was shot is the day I was kidnapped. "Oh." I push my food away, because suddenly I'm not that hungry. "So, you two are pretty close?"

"Yeah, I'd say so."

"And you're not—" How do I ask this without sounding like a jerk?

Jelly wipes her hands on a napkin and then scoots her chair next to mine. "What is it, Win?"

"Aren't you afraid that the next enemy will come?" I take a

deep breath to help calm my nerves. "Aren't you afraid that they'll put your life at risk again?"

Jelly wraps her arm around me. "Of course, I worry some." Then she leans her head on mine. "But honestly, Win, those dangers are out there with or without the Iron Devils. Motorcycle Clubs aren't the only source of danger. Evil lurks around every corner."

She's right. I could get held at gunpoint at the ATM or be in the crossfire at some major event. Because I need to know, I ask. "Have you heard from Fang?"

Sitting ramrod straight, she asks, "You haven't listened to the million messages he's left on your voicemail?"

Guilt washes over me. I know I should play those messages. Hear him out. It's just that my heart wasn't ready. I'm not sure it's ready now, or if it ever will be. All I know is that in that short time, I got to know Fang, I fell for him. I fell harder for him than I did for Billy. "I couldn't."

"Girl." Jelly grips my shoulders and gives them a good shake. "That man has got it bad. He asks about you every time I step foot in the clubhouse. He doesn't attend parties or hang out with any of his club members. All he does is sulk in his room."

Jeez, that sounds exactly like me. I have not left this house since I came home two weeks ago. The most I socialize is when Jelly comes to do her check-ins. Seems we are two miserable peas in a pod.

"Don't let fear get in the way of love."

My eyes widen at her use of the word love. "Whoa, nobody said anything about love. Hell, we only had a short time together, and most of that time was spent apart."

"Please." Jelly smiles. "Time has nothing to do with love. Sometimes love takes months to develop." She squeezes my arm. "Other times it's instant."

"You can't honestly tell me that you believe in insta-love." I can't even say that I believe in love at first sight.

Jelly giggles. "Sometimes the best things in life are those that we instantly fall in love with. Tell me I'm wrong."

I can't tell her she's wrong because I instantly fell in love with Olaf, the cat I found on the side of the street at age nine. He was my everything. Until his final breath. Could this thing between Fang and me be love? Is he my happily ever after?

CHAPTER TWENTY-FIVE

Fang

I'm miserable. Life sucks donkey balls, and there's no end in sight. Every day I leave Winter a voicemail, hoping she'll call me back. Let me know how she's doing, even if she doesn't want me like I want her.

There's a knock on my bedroom door. "Go away, Sinner, I'm not hungry." I swear that man is worse than any mom portrayed on TV.

A key is inserted, and the knob twists. I'm about to start swearing at my uncle when a lean blonde walks in carrying a greasy bag from Mick's. "Sandra, what are you doing here?" The words come out harsher than I mean. Seems my foul mood knows no bounds.

"Well, aren't you full of unicorn farts and zombie

bubblegum?" She closes the door behind her and tosses the brown paper bag my way.

I barely catch it in time. When I open it, I see Mick's famous bacon-and-avocado double cheeseburger with an extra side of fries. Even though I'm not hungry, my stomach sounds off like I haven't eaten in years.

Tossing a fry in my mouth, I glare at my friend. "Unicorn farts and zombie bubblegum?" I shake my head because that is the stupidest thing I have ever heard. Well, that's not entirely true. Sandra is known for her weird sense of humor.

"Listen, I heard about Winter." Sandra folds her hands in front of her, shifting weight from foot-to-foot. I wish she would stop, it's grating on my nerves.

"Yeah." Tossing the bag on the bedside table, I stand, making my way to the door. "I really don't feel like talking about it."

Opening the door, I motion for her to leave. Instead, she traipses over to my bed and sits. Slamming the door, I cross my arms over my chest. "What do you want, Sandra. I'm not in the mood for company."

"I don't care if you're in the mood or not. I'm here." She pats the spot next to her. "You may as well come over here and talk."

If it hadn't been for the fact that Sandra was my rock when my brother died, I most likely wouldn't allow her to talk to me this way. Because I know she understands how I feel, and this comes from a good place, I'll take it.

Snagging the bag, I sit on what is now, and always will be, Winter's side. Leaning against the headboard, I pull the contents out of the bag. Flattening the paper bag, I dump the fries on top and start chowing down. The salty potatoes are just what I needed.

"Fang, Sinner is worried about you." She places her hand on my shoulder. "All of them are."

I roll my eyes.

"Look, I'm sure facing off with Ghost was terrible. That man is responsible for taking Vile away from us, but he's dead. All the Hollow Bones are dead."

"Just stop." I'm so tired of thinking about Ghost and how he was Winter's uncle. A man whom she apparently looked up to as a kid. Now I'm just the monster that put him in an early grave. Well, technically, it was Ramon who put a bullet in Ghost.

"Fang, Dad told me about Ghost being Winter's uncle. How he tortured her just to get back at you."

"Sandra, thank you for the food, but you need to get the hell out of here. Now." Why does everyone find it necessary to keep bringing up Ghost and Winter? My brain just needs a little rest.

"No." She stands from the bed. "I'm not going anywhere. You're hurting and you need a friend to set you straight."

"Oh, you're gonna set me straight, are ya?" I shove several fries into my mouth to keep from saying things I shouldn't.

"Yeah, I am." She stomps over to the side I'm currently sitting on, knocking fries out of my hand. "You're being a grade A jerk."

"Yeah, well, I didn't ask you."

Sandra grips my face in both hands. "Fang." She forces my gaze to hers. "Fight for her."

"I am not going to force my way into Winter's life."

"I'm not suggesting you force her to take you back."
Sandra's tone softens. "You love her. For the first time in your
life, you found true love."

"That's absurd." I shove her hands away. "We barely know
each other."

"Barely knowing each other does not make it any less
true." She snags a fry. "You love her, now go fight for her."

Standing, I jab a finger at her. "You're a real pain in the
ass, you know that?"

Sandra laughs. "So, I've been told." She starts picking up
my discarded food. "Now go get your girl, I'll clean up." Wrin-
kling her nose, she adds, "Maybe I'll change your sheets and
light a candle, it stinks to high heaven in here."

"Whatever." I wad the napkin in my hand and toss it at
her. She's not wrong, though. I have not opened a window or
freshened up my room since the day Winter walked out,
claiming she couldn't deal with this life.

Jogging down the stairs, all talking stops when they see
who it is. I don't even care that they were talking about me.
Let them. Not saying a word, I walk out the front door and
hop on my bike.

The roar is a soothing balm.

I have never been to Winter's house before, but I do have
the address memorized. As I exit the compound gate, I get a
good look at the house across the street. The house Ghost
sent us to so they could ambush us.

Now it's just a pile of ashes. After we rescued Winter and
killed all the Hollow Bones, Sinner and Ramon carried Ghost
and Rat across the road. Dumped their bodies amongst their
friends and lit the place on fire.

Turning left, I ride the streets. Wind blowing in my hair. It feels good to be back on my bike. I didn't realize how much I missed her. Missed the roar and wind. The vibration makes my bones come alive. Blood flows smoothly when I'm riding her.

When I pull into Winter's driveway, I notice Jelly's car. Good, that means my girl hasn't been alone. She's had her friend here checking up on her. Dismounting my bike, I startle when the front door swings open.

Winter is standing in the doorway, keys in hand. "Fang, what are you doing here?"

Maybe I should have called. She's clearly on her way out with her friend. I hang my helmet on the handlebars. "I came to see you, but if you're busy—"

"No." She tosses her keys in her purse and sets the black bag on a table nearby. "Don't leave, I was actually on my way to see you."

This gives me pause. I thought she didn't want anything to do with me because of the dangers of the club. "You were on your way to see me?" I ask dumbly.

"Yes." She takes a tentative step toward me.

"To return my pillow?" Why do I say that? I don't know. Now that it's left my mouth, I feel like an idiot.

"No." She bites her bottom lip and glances over my shoulder like she's shy. "I mean, I can run up and grab your pillow, I'm sure you want it back." Winter turns like she's about to escape. Jelly steps up behind her and grips her shoulders, turning her back around.

"Truthfully," I say as I make my way toward her. "I would much rather have you back. The pillow can be replaced."

Her hazel eyes lock with mine. "Really?"

"Yes, really." I take her hands. "Winter Mynt Green, you stole my heart the minute you planted your lips on mine at the Halloween Carnival. One night full of haunts and treats turned out to be the night I found my forever."

"I love you." Winter jumps in my arms, locking her legs around my waist, and kissing me like she hasn't tasted me in centuries.

"Well, my work here is done." Jelly steps around us. "Y'all go inside and tarnish those fresh sheets. I'll lock up."

Neither of us comes up for air to say bye to Jelly. As I carry Winter up to her room, I hear the door close and a car drive away.

It's not hard to find Winter's room. Once I reach the top of the stairs, I see a bedroom with bookshelves lining the farthest wall. Stepping over the threshold, I see it. My pillow. It sticks out like a sore thumb with a black pillowcase. The rest of her bedding is a lavender color with a butterfly print.

"Is this what you want?" There is no way in hell I'm assuming sex is on the table. If she wants it, she'll get it. Otherwise, I will wait.

"These last couple of weeks, I thought I might die without you." Winter kisses my neck. Licks behind my ear. "I want you, Ezra Armstrong." It's been a long time since I've been called by my birth name, and it sounds damn good coming from her mouth.

Untangling her legs from my waist, Winter eases out of my hold. Her hands slip under my cut, dragging it over my shoulders. Once she has it off, she tosses it on her bedside table. I love the fact that she didn't just haphazardly toss it to the floor.

With achingly slow speed, she lifts my shirt over my head, leaving wet kisses in its wake. "Shouldn't I be the one teasing you?"

"No." Tossing my shirt to the floor, she licks one nipple, then the other. "See, you left me wanting that day you rode off."

Gripping a handful of hair, I force her to look at me. "I didn't leave you that way on purpose." Smashing my lips to hers, I kiss her with all the passion left in me. She tastes of mint. "I simply didn't want our first time to be because I might die." I pull a little tighter on her strands. "I wanted to worship you the way you deserve. Take my time with you."

Her back arches, and her breathing grows heavy. "Please."

I grin because I know I have her right where I want her. "Please, what, Winter?"

"Please." This time it's a whisper.

With one hand, I unzip her jeans and work them down her legs. My other hand keeps a tight grip on her hair, holding her in place. Lazily, my gaze travels up her thighs. They have a slight tremble to them. I wonder how long it's been since she's been loved the right way. The way her body so easily responds to my touch tells me that her past lovers were very insufficient.

Releasing her hair, I lift her into my arms only to lay her on the bed. Before she can move, I grip her lace panties and rip them down the side. She gasps but doesn't say a word, just lifts her hips when I tug the remaining fabric down her leg.

"Don't move." I bend over to untie my boots. Placing

them under the bed, I take my time removing the denim from my body. Winter's eyes watch my every move. Wetness glistens between her legs. "You ready for me, baby?"

Biting that bottom lip, she nods. If I weren't so desperate to sink balls deep into her, I would make her use her words. Truth be told, I don't think I can wait another second. Crawling onto the bed, I press my lips to hers. She immediately opens for me. We kiss wildly, our bodies pressing impossibly closer. I need to be in her.

Grabbing hold of her leg, I lift it over my hip, then align myself with her core. She's so tight that sweat is dotting my forehead. I may need to switch our positions. Put her on top so she can open up better.

Just as I prepare to flip her, she lifts her other leg and flexes her hips. The new angle allows me to slide in. It's still a tight fit, but damn does she feel amazing. "God, baby, you feel so good."

Lifting her head, she bites my shoulder, groaning in ecstasy. If she keeps that up, I won't last long. Hell, I may not last long anyway. It's been forever since I've been with a woman. Reaching between us, I find her clit and gently rub circles.

Throwing her head back, she cries out. Body thrashing. Hot damn, this woman is stunning when she comes. Not to mention she came so easily for me. Which brings me back to my original thought. Her previous lovers were shit in bed.

"Honey, I'm home," Jelly yells as she enters my house.

"In here." I'm in the office, replying to my editor about my newest book. It's the one I wrote last year after my kidnapping. All the final touches have been made, and the publisher is ready to get it on the market.

Jelly enters and gasps. "Girlfriend, where is your costume?"

"I told you I didn't want to go out. Besides, Fang is taking off early to take me out for my birthday."

Jelly giggles like she's got some inside joke. "Yeah, there's been a change of plans."

"Hell no." I shake my head. "You remember what happened last year?"

My best friend nods. There's no way she doesn't remember. It affected her as much as it did me. "The Hollow Bones are dead and gone." Embracing me in the tightest hug ever, she squeals, "You have an announcement to make, and tonight at the Halloween Carnival will be the perfect time."

To match Fang, Jelly bought me a black dress with black angel wings. A fallen angel for a fallen angel. I dress up and follow her out the door.

When we arrive, Snake greets us at the gate. "Hey, babe."

Jelly kisses him. "Hey."

"Winter." He nods at me, and I wave. Over the last year, I have gotten to know the Iron Devils. They have all become like family to me. "Fang is over by the hayride, waitin' for ya."

Jelly loops her arm with mine and practically skips toward the horse and wagon. Fang is standing next to the carriage, talking with Sinner. When they hear our footsteps, both men turn around. Fang's eyes light up like a kid on Christmas morning. Just like last year, he is wearing jeans and black angel wings, no shirt.

Just like last year, my breath catches when I get that first glimpse of him. Wolf and Ramon emerge from the shadows. Footsteps behind us have me turning to see Snake jogging to catch up.

I raise a brow in question, and Fang beckons me over. As I reach Fang, Sinner steps aside, hands clasped in front of him. Fang takes my hand and kneels. Surely, he isn't doing what I think he's doing. "Winter, from the moment I met you, I knew you were the one. Would you do me the honor and marry me?"

Everyone is staring at me, waiting with anticipation. Smiling down at Fang, I say, "Yes."

He slips the diamond on my finger and jumps up with a shout.

"Calm down, lover." I take him by the hand. "I have an announcement of my own." Jelly squeals, clapping her hands in excitement. She's known this secret for the last week.

Fang gives her the side eye, then takes my other hand. "What is it?"

I place one of his hands on my belly. "You're gonna be a daddy."

With eyes wide, he stares down at my flat stomach. "You mean, there's a little Armstrong in there?"

"That's exactly what I mean."

Sinner, Wolf, Ramon, and Snake all hoot and holler. Sinner gets on his radio and announces to the rest of the Iron Devils. "She said yes. I repeat, she said yes. Also, she's got a bun in the oven."

"You've just made me the happiest man alive." Fang cups my face and kisses me so tenderly, tears spring to my eyes. I've read that these new emotions I've been experiencing are due to hormones. I hope it passes soon. Crying over hotdog commercials is downright embarrassing.

"I love you, Ezra."

"I love you, Winter."

MEET THE GANG

Elise Gedicke – Witch Upon a Star

Erin Osborne – Outlawed Treat

Amy Davies – War's Witch

Calia Wilde – Roses are Dead

Jasmine Grant – Runt's Haunted Ride

Sydney Aaliyah Michelle – Point of Infinity

Penny Anglene – Crane's Hallowed Wrath

Quinn Ryder – Haunting Phantom

Jules Ford – The Devil's Hour

Tich Brewster – Fang

Cala Riley – The Devil's Den

Winter Travers – Claimed by Werewolf

TEAM MOBSTERS

Kathleen Kelly – Graveyard Promises

Elle Boon – Hunting Savage

Heather Dahlgren – Halloween Hit

JL Quincy – The Devil's Masked Corruption

Nola Marie – L'amore del Diavolo

D Williams – Trick or Threat

Harley Wylde – Devil's Embrace

Andi Lynn – Haunting the Shadow Man

ER Whyte – Haunt Me With Vengeance

Ruby Carter – Vows and Vendettas

T.O. Smith – Slay Tricksters and Silent Skeletons

Avelyn Paige – The Reaper's Vow

Cleo Browne – Dima's Vision

Dove Cavanaugh King – Samhain Savior

Eve R. Hart – Cursed Encounter

Glenna Maynard – Wicked Vows

H.J. Marshall – The Madman's Nightmare

Sammie Lyra – His Wicked Spell

Kristine Allen – Broomsticks and Bloodstains

Annelise Reynolds – Traitor or Treat

Rae B. Lake – Haunted Nights & Savage Sins

Lynne Leslie – Blood, Bones, and The Bratva Bogeyman

Layne Daniels – Bratva Beast's Boo

E.C. Land – Bloodmoon Hit

PLAYLIST

The Animals – House of the Rising Sun
Citizen Soldier – I'm Not Okay
Eminem – Lose Yourself
Eminem – Till I Collapse
EMO – Dancing with the Devil
Matt Maeson – Dancing After Death
Murcielago – Don't Do Nothin'
NF – Lost in the Moment
Skillet – Awake and Alive
Skillet – Monster
Skillet – Not Gonna Die
Smash Into Pieces – All Eyes on You
Victor Ray – Comfortable
Yelawolf – Devil in my Veins
Yelawolf – Till It's Gone

instagram.com/tichbrewster

facebook.com/TichBrewsterAuthor

tiktok.com/@tichbrewster

x.com/TichBrewster